WHALE BOY

www.randomhousechildrens.co.uk

Also by Nicola Davies:

A Girl Called Dog
Rubbish Town Hero

WHALE BOY

NICOLA DAVIES

CORGI YEARLING

WHALE BOY
A CORGI YEARLING BOOK 978 0 440 87015 9

First published in Great Britain by Corgi Yearling,
an imprint of Random House Children's Publishers UK
A Random House Group Company

This edition published 2013

5 7 9 10 8 6 4

Text copyright © Nicola Davies, 2013
Artwork © Joe McLaren, 2013

The Random House Group Limited supports the Forest Stewardship Council® (FSC®),
the leading international forest-certification organisation. Our books carrying the FSC
label are printed on FSC®-certified paper. FSC is the only forest-certification scheme
supported by the leading environmental organisations, including Greenpeace. Our paper
procurement policy can be found at www.randomhouse.co.uk/environment.

MIX
Paper from
responsible sources
FSC® C016897

Set in Goudy Old Style

RANDOM HOUSE CHILDREN'S PUBLISHERS UK
61–63 Uxbridge Road, London W5 5SA

www.randomhousechildrens.co.uk
www.totallyrandombooks.co.uk
www.randomhouse.co.uk

Addresses for companies within The Random House Group Limited can be found at:
www.randomhouse.co.uk/offices.htm

THE RANDOM HOUSE GROUP Limited Reg. No. 954009

A CIP catalogue record for this book is available from the British Library.

Printed and bound in Great Britain by
CPI Group (UK) LTD, Croydon, CR0 4YY

For Hal and the crew of
Firenze, *Elendil* and *Baleana*,
with love and thanks.

There's a place where the water runs deep enough to lose the highest mountain. That's where the whales come. So many you can walk on their backs.

And here's how to find it . . .

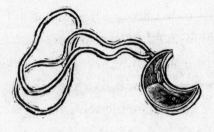

1

All day Michael stared out of the window. The ocean peeped at him from between the houses on the bay. That sliver of blue was like a promise. 'I'm here,' it said, 'waiting for you!'

Of course it got him into trouble, like always: Mrs Matthews told him off for daydreaming, and Mr Damou made him stay in at lunch time and write *I must pay attention in school* fifty times on the blackboard. Eugenia, who had sat next to him in class since first grade, wagged her finger at him. 'You'll never amount to anything, Michael Fontaine,' she scolded, 'if all you think of is the sea!'

Michael didn't answer her. What did Eugenia know? She wanted to be a lawyer, or a doctor, or a president – something *shut inside a building*. She didn't know what it was like to be out on the sea. She didn't know how the waves whisper on a hot day, or how the dolphins ride your bow as you skim through the swells. She didn't know about the place where the whales were.

There's a place where the water runs deep enough to lose the highest mountain. That's where the whales come. So many you can walk on their backs . . .

Michael's father, Samuel, had told him this just before he went away. Most of the time the whales wandered the wide oceans, but sometimes they swarmed in waters close to land.

'And *this* tells you how to find them,' he had said, putting a silver medallion around Michael's neck. It was shaped like a new moon, with the head of a sperm whale on it. Samuel had read the tiny words etched in the silver because Michael had been too small to read very well.

When Peter hides the Devil and . . .

4

'It's half of a riddle,' Samuel had told him.

'But where's the other half?' Michael exclaimed in disappointment.

His father shrugged. 'I think my grandpa gave the other half to my big brother Davis.'

'So what did the words on Uncle Davis's half say?' Michael had asked.

'I don't know, son. Uncle Davis and I weren't close, and he kept his medallion out of sight, so I never found out what it said.' Then he laughed at his son's solemn face. 'But it's just an old story, anyway. Nothin' will work to find whales now; they were hunted out around the island long ago.'

Michael had known with his head that his father was right, the whales *had* gone. But in his heart he had wondered, if the sea was so big, could whales still be hidden somewhere, and come back to the waters around Liberty? Samuel had just smiled his big warm smile and said, 'I hope it keeps you safe, son, even if it's no good for finding whales.'

Now Michael touched the medallion through his shirt. He always kept it hidden, as if bringing it into the light would make the memory of his father and the idea of whales fade to nothing.

Whether or not there were whales still in the ocean, Michael longed to be out *on* it, free under the sky. But to do that, you needed a boat, and today was the day when he was finally going to get one. Just like the sea, it was waiting for him. It had been waiting for three years, but from today, it wouldn't have to wait any longer. Now it would be his to go wherever he pleased – across the bay to catch fish or the whole way to the horizon. All he had to do was wait for school to be over, then he could escape.

The moment the bell sounded, he was off. He dodged across the playground and out of the gate. The other children watched him go and shrugged: that Michael Fontaine was a mystery – he never seemed to talk to anyone in school and he was *always* rushing somewhere.

Michael ran across the park, between the

talipot palms and the frangipani trees. He didn't stop to watch the tiny emerald hummingbirds dashing amongst the hibiscus blossoms, but raced straight out onto the Old Town road, which ran around the bay. He ran past the little wooden houses and the shops with homemade signs, and the gaps between them where the beach and the ocean showed through. Taxis and buses jostled along in the Friday afternoon heat – children going home from school, tourists heading inland to the mountains, grown-ups finishing work early. Girls perched in doorways plaiting their hair and painting their nails. On the pavement, old ladies on picnic chairs sold mangoes from carrier bags, and a skinny fisherman chopped up a huge tuna with a machete, like someone doing a conjuring trick. Calypso music danced out of open windows, and it felt like the whole of Rose Town was already in holiday mood, although it was just an ordinary weekend and Carnival was still a few weeks away.

Everyone was in a good mood, and Michael's many employers greeted him as they saw him running past. Mr Rooseveldt Dringo, whose bus, *De Truth*, Michael washed every Sunday night, honked his horn and whistled. 'Mikey! Why you in such a big rush?'

Miss Eliza Harmany, the proprietor of Gifted Hands Unisex Hair Salon, blew kisses. 'Hey, Michael, you coming to sweep up for me Tuesday?'

But only Mr Errol Joseph, owner of the Flying Fish Frizzle Bar and Restaurant, got any more than a smile and a wave out of Michael as he rushed along.

'Michael!' he called out. 'Can you work tonight?'

Michael stopped in the shade of the awning. 'Sure, Mr Joseph,' he panted.

'Ah, Michael. I knew I could rely on you. Can I get you an iced tea? Wanna seat?'

'Not right now, Mr Joseph. I'm on my way to put the next down payment on my boat!'

'So *that's* why you in such a rush!' Mr Joseph smiled. 'How long you been savin' now, Mikey?'

'Three years,' he replied proudly.

Mr Joseph shook the boy's hand solemnly. 'Respect to you, Mikey!' he said. 'You'll be catching fish like your father did any day now!'

'Maybe tomorrow!' Michael grinned. 'Mr Levi said I could take the boat when I'd paid half of the price. And this' – he patted the money in his pocket – 'makes up the half!'

Mr Joseph's face clouded. 'D'you mean Edison Levi? At the yard next to the fish market?'

The grim look on Mr Joseph's face made Michael's mouth go dry. He nodded without speaking.

Mr Joseph shook his head in dismay. 'Oh Mikey! You better get down there. They're putting some big old fence round the whole place, shuttin' everyone out.'

Michael didn't wait to ask any more. He flew along past the public baths, the radio station and the library, through the one smart bit of town where a few swanky hotels looked out to sea, and down to the seafront. He felt as if his feet weren't even touching the hot concrete as he sped round

9

the corner of the fish market and went smack into the taut steel mesh of a huge pair of gates. A sign said:

KEEP OUT!
NEW MARINE ENTERPRISES –
BRINGING PROSPERITY FROM THE OCEAN TO THE
REPUBLIC OF LIBERTY:
ROSE TOWN QUAY REDEVELOPMENT PROGRAMME AND
MARINE EXHIBITION CENTRE

Edison Levi's shack had stood at the corner of the fish market for ever. His stock of scruffy canoes and battered rowing boats had gathered alongside like a little flock of ragged seagulls, among them the boat that Michael had come to think of as his own. It was not much bigger than a table top, and its blue fibreglass was whiskery from age and sun, rather like Mr Levi himself. But it didn't leak and it was easy to row. It was his start in the world; the first step towards having a boat big enough to take people out fishing and dolphin spotting, the way he and his dad had always planned. From the moment he set eyes on it, Michael had loaded it with a cargo of dreams.

Mr Levi had kept a careful record of every one of Michael's down payments in the red notebook that he stored under the cushion of his rocking chair. Only two days ago he had said, 'Another twenty dollars, Mikey, and you can start to use her. Once you're catching fish you'll pay off the rest in no time. Hey, I'll even throw in a fish trap!'

But there was no sign of Edison Levi now. Men in hard hats were flinging the splintered remains of his shack into a huge skip, where fragments of boat stuck up like teeth. The blue prow of Michael's boat poked out at one end, its broken stern at the other. Michael laced his fingers through the wire fence and stared in horror.

'Where's Mr Levi?' he yelled out to the workmen.

One of them walked towards him, scowling. 'Go 'way!' he growled. He had a strong accent that made his words sound unfamiliar.

'D'you know where Mr Levi's gone?' Michael asked.

'*Infierno?*' The man shrugged, then banged the wire. 'You go now!'

'Did you find a book – a red notebook?' Michael persisted.

The man smiled nastily and pulled the little book from the pocket of his overalls. 'This? No, I no find.'

Michael felt himself turn cold as the man flung Mr Levi's notebook into the water and walked away, laughing.

The pages scattered over the surface and the cheap paper was immediately soaked through. In moments all record of Michael's three years of hard-earned payments had sunk to the bottom of the harbour.

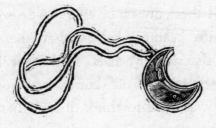

2

All the way back along the Old Town road Michael's outside smiled at people and greeted them politely. But inside, disappointment and anger swirled like a hurricane, a storm so fierce that he hardly knew what his outside was doing. When he finally noticed where he was, he found he was standing on Cat's Paw Beach, the little strand just out of town, near his grandmother's house.

A slap on the shoulder brought his inside and outside properly back together. It was So-So, who had been his father's friend and had taught him about boats and fishing after Samuel's own father, Michael's grandpa, Ivor, had drowned in a storm.

'Ah! Michael, my star brother!' So-So exclaimed with a huge beaming smile and another slap on the back that made Michael's teeth rattle. Michael knew So-So must be old, but he was so spry and strong it was hard to think of him that way. It was only So-So's brain that didn't work so well these days; perhaps never had. Michael's gran said that So-So had been born with a mind that was 'visiting the cherubs'. Once he had had a little house and a boat and fished every day, but somehow he'd lost them both. Then he'd helped in Samuel's boat, and now he lived under a tree on the beach. He wore all sorts of strange things that he found as clothing – today, a threadbare orange beach towel as a skirt and a long necklace made from the ring pulls from drinks cans.

He stood in front of Michael and looked intently into his face. 'Your heart is troubled, my brother star!' he said. 'I know it!'

So-So might visit angels and wear trash as jewellery, but Michael's dad had always said that he saw things other people didn't.

He rested a big hand on Michael's shoulder. 'Be not troubled, my star brother,' he said. 'You are growing into a strong man and the sun shall not smite you by day, nor the moon by night. Not while So-So is here, you father's friend.'

There was a sadness in So-So's eyes that made it hard to hold his gaze, but there was a calmness too. Michael felt the hurricane inside die down. He sighed.

'Better, better!' said So-So, nodding. 'You are like your father – one moment sunlight and the next shadow, one moment storm and the next calm. But now you are peaceful, see? We will fish! Pascal says the fish are in the bay.'

He pointed to the far end of the beach, where a little knot of people had formed around a net, and handed Michael a face mask and snorkel; Michael smiled at his father's old friend, and together they ran down the beach to join the fishing party.

Pascal Loubière had been fishing Cat's Paw Bay for fifty years. He spent his days playing dominoes with his cronies in a hut overlooking the beach so he could watch the water and the sky. He could tell, like no one else, when there were fish to be caught. So when Mr Loubière asked for help with his net, you knew it would be worth your while. Michael trod water while Mr Loubière, So-So and five other regular helpers waded up to their chests to spread the net in an arc across the cove. It was good to be in the water. Floating here, with the green heights of the island billowing up above the town, and the ocean cradling his body, he felt better: Gran would know where to find old Mr Levi; he would get his down payments back; he would buy another boat somewhere else.

Mr Loubière waved, and Michael put the mask over his face and dived. Suspended in the water between the softly gleaming sand and the crinkled brightness of the surface was a big shoal of ballyhoo, like a woven basket of silver threads, moving this way and that in the water. Michael swam towards them, coaxing them between Mr Loubière's helpers, and within the line of the net. This wasn't as good as being out at sea in a boat, but it would do for now.

As Michael wriggled his damp body back into his clothes, So-So gave him half of his own share of the catch, and a plastic bucket to carry the fish in. 'Don't want to be like some bong-belly pikny,' he said, patting his stomach. 'Only need enough to eat and buy some smokes.'

Michael tried to thank him, but So-So just waved his hands in front of his face, and backed away down the beach, laughing. 'You are creation stepper, my brother star,' he called out. 'You are sun and dark – you walk the world of trouble with no fear.'

It was the perfect time to be selling fresh fish. People were hurrying home and looking for something for supper. Almost at once an old green car drew up alongside the pavement where Michael stood with his bucket. A lady in sunglasses smiled out at him.

'Michael! How are you?'

It was Eugenia's mother. Eugenia was in the back seat with her baby brother, Mostyn. She looked at him disapprovingly, as always.

'I'm good, thanks, Mrs Thomson. You want some fish?'

'I do indeed. In fact you've just saved us from having nothing but rice for supper. I'll take all you have.'

'Fine. I just need to keep some back for my gran.'

'Of course.' Mrs Thomson handed over a five-dollar bill.

'You want to take the bucket for the fish, Mrs Thomson?' Michael asked. 'I've got a little bag for my gran's.'

'Oh, that's kind, Michael,' she said. 'I'll get Eugenia to bring it to the Flying Fish tonight.'

Michael's face showed his astonishment.

'So I guess you didn't know?' Mrs Thomson laughed and turned round to Eugenia. 'Tell Michael about your new job, Eugenia!'

Eugenia was fussing with her baby brother's hair and spoke without looking at him. 'I'm going to wait tables for Mr Joseph,' she said.

'She saving to put herself through college,' Mrs

Thomson told him proudly. Eugenia said nothing
– she just carried on making sure her brother's
perfectly white socks were folded down just the
same on each foot. *Poor kid*, Michael thought. *He
can't get away from her wanting everything in straight
lines.*

'Thanks for the fish, Michael!' said her
mother.

'No problem, Mrs Thomson!' Michael smiled
his best businessman's smile, and waved as the car
coughed and grumbled its way into the traffic.

Saving for college indeed! Michael punched
the fence of the Morning Glory Bakery and made
its boards ring. Now he would have Eugenia's
nagging all evening as well as all day. Still, the
thought of Eugenia eating fish that he'd caught
was almost enough to put a spring back in his
step. *I may not amount to much in your eyes, Eugenia
Thomson*, he said to himself, *but your belly would be
growling tonight if it weren't for me!*

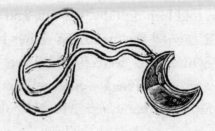

3

The sun was sinking as Michael ran home, and on the last bend he almost bumped into someone in the fading light. It was Gran, on her way back from her job in the Shiny Row Laundry in town. Even though she was older than the hills, she kept on working.

'Nobody's gonna look out for you and me, my boy,' she always said, 'so we got to do it for our own selves.'

Gran had been looking out for Michael for most of his life, since his mum had gone back to England when he was a tiny baby. His mum came from an old Liberty family – back in the whaling

20

days they had been harpooners – but had moved to London when she was very small. She had met Michael's father when she'd returned to Liberty for a visit one year at Carnival time; Samuel thought they'd always live together on the island.

'She just wasn't mother material,' was all Gran could ever be persuaded to say about her. Michael didn't even know what his mother looked like – there wasn't a single photograph of her anywhere. But she must have been pretty, because in the end Dad had decided to leave Liberty and join his older brother Davis in England so he could look for his wife. He'd sold his fishing boat to pay for the ticket. That was six years ago now, almost seven, and they hadn't heard a word from him since. At first Gran had written a few letters to an address in London, but Samuel had never written back.

Michael remembered their last day together, fishing far from shore, making plans to buy a bigger boat, maybe take tourists out on trips.

'Who knows, Michael,' his father had said.

'Maybe we could find some of the old whales to show 'em, eh?'

After he left, Michael had wondered about the whales, and what Samuel had told him.

'Do you remember the whales around the island?' he'd asked Gran.

'Oh my goodness, yes!' she'd said, her eyes wide. 'When I was little, a few ships still came into harbour with the barrels of whale oil on their decks. Your great-grandfather, Grandpa's daddy, he worked on a whale boat when he was a boy, up in the crow's nest, watching for spouts! He was a champion whale-finder, Ivor always used to say.'

Gran had never seen a live whale, but she'd seen their bones.

'Big as rocks, they were, sunk in the bottom of the harbour. All rotted away now, though, I expect. The only bones left are in that hotel where the rich people stay.' She shook her head sadly. 'It's a shame and disgrace that we killed those great creatures, that's *my* opinion!'

Gran had been right about the bones. Michael's

school teacher took the class to see the sperm whale skeleton in the foyer of the Rathborne Hotel in town. It was painted white and bigger than the inside of Gran's house. So big, it was impossible to imagine it had been inside a living body, a body that swam and floated in the sea. Even Eugenia, who never cared about anything but books and learning, was impressed.

'I wish there were *still* whales!' she'd sighed, and was quiet for a whole *fifteen minutes*.

So at least Samuel hadn't been making it all up, but nobody had seen a whale spout anywhere near the island in half a century. They were just a story now, something not quite real any more, like Michael's father.

Even though the whales and his father had gone, Michael decided that he could still make *real* plans: he would work hard and get a boat of his own, and go back out onto the sea.

Gran didn't like boats and she didn't want him to go out on the sea. After her husband drowned – his boat had disappeared in a hurricane when

Samuel was tiny – the sea had always scared her. She'd never liked Samuel and Michael going out fishing. So because Michael loved his gran and didn't want her to worry, he didn't tell her about his plans or why he worked so hard and saved his money so carefully.

Life had been very tough for Gran. She was the only person in Michael's whole family who hadn't been busy leaving the country or dying.

'I'm durable,' she used to tell him when he was small. 'That means I'll *last* for a long, long time, so I can *always* take care of you.'

But she had begun to look far from durable. Coming across her in the dusk, Michael noticed once again how *small* she was. He had been taller than her for more than a year. She was tiny and fragile; now *she* needed *his* protection.

'Goodness me!' Gran exclaimed. 'You gave me a fright there, Ivor.'

Lately, she had started calling him by the wrong name. At first he'd complained to her, but she got so upset that he began to ignore it, so as not to

24

hurt her feelings. After all, the names weren't *any* old wrong names, but names of other people in his family.

Usually it was Ivor. Sometimes it was Davis, the name of her elder son. 'He was wild, that boy,' Gran would say, shaking her head. He'd gone to London to drive a taxi, while his younger brother Samuel was still in school – long before Michael was born. He didn't write or visit either, but Gran always got a card from him at Christmas.

And sometimes Gran would call Michael by his father's name. It hurt every time she did it because it was the only time they mentioned Samuel these days. Somehow they'd both stopped talking about him.

'Oh!' Gran put down her bags. Michael couldn't help noticing how big they looked compared to her. She clapped a hand to her mouth. 'Did I just call you Ivor? I must be losing my mind.'

'No, Gran,' Michael reassured her, 'you didn't. You're sharp as a tack. Hey! Gimme those bags.'

'I can carry my own bags!' she said. Gran never

liked to rely on anyone. *Don't rely on another soul,*
then you don't owe nobody a thing was one of her
many favourite sayings. But Michael picked up her
bags anyway and she didn't argue. They walked
on in silence while the sun finished sinking. The
velvet-soft dark crept out from under the trees by
the side of the road as they reached the rickety
little gate into their front garden. It creaked and
grumbled open, and Gran began to climb the
steep, narrow path under the grapefruit trees.

'So, why were you running so hard, Ivo— I
mean, Michael?' Gran wheezed as she plonked
herself down on the bench on the veranda. 'You
near run me down. Something the matter, eh?'

In some ways, Michael thought, Gran really *was*
still as sharp as a tack. She could tell when something was wrong, even if he tried not to show it.

'I'm fine,' he lied, 'and I have fish for your
supper.'

Michael took the bags inside and lit the Tilley
lamp. He put the fish on a plate under a flyscreen
and went back out to sit beside her. Gran knew

26

all the old people in Rose Town. *She* would know where to find old Mr Levi and get his down-payment money back. But he had to be careful, or she would wonder why he was asking about him. Now wasn't the right time to reveal his boat plans. So he did his best to sound as casual as possible when he asked, 'You seen that big old fence they put up next to the fish market?'

Gran's eyes grew wide. 'I *have*,' she said. 'I have indeed. And d'you know old Edison Levi? Had a little business next to the market? You maybe didn't know him, but I was at school with that boy's sister, Marietta. The New Marine Enterprises people – they took his shack and his boats – just took 'em, like that!' She snapped her fingers. 'And he dropped dead on the spot. *Dead!* That business was all he had. No wife, no children. Just that. It's a scandal.'

Michael was glad he was sitting down.

'You sure you fine, Michael?' Gran asked.

He managed to nod, to say that he had to get to work. Even made a joke about saving to take her on a cruise ship, which made her laugh. 'Wouldn't catch me on one of them floating skyscrapers,' she said.

Then he changed out of his school uniform and walked back into town, with his heart heavy as a rock in his chest.

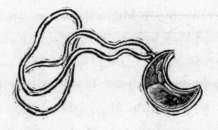

4

The Flying Fish Frizzle Bar was full of Friday night customers. Michael came in through the back door to find the cooks, Xavier and Vernon, already yelling at each other like they always did when things got really crazy. Out in the restaurant, Mr Joseph was busy serving behind the bar, and the waitresses, Malady and Julietta, were whizzing around taking orders. There was no sign of Eugenia at first, and then she came in through the swing door, pushing it open with her bottom, her tray loaded with dirty dishes.

'These are for you, Michael Fontaine,' she said, dumping the loaded tray by the sink. 'Enjoy!'

Her smirk made Michael furious. He decided not to even look at her, and just set to work.

Deafened by the clatter of pots and swirled in steam and water, Michael thought about the notebook at the bottom of the harbour, the blue boat snapped in two, and poor Mr Levi, dead as a fish. The sign on the new fence didn't mean a thing. New Marine Enterprises was a company, not a real person you could write to and say, *Why did you bust my boat and where are my down payments?* Michael had washed *so* many dirty dishes to earn that money – they would surely make a pile as big as a mountain range. Now he would have to wash them all over again to make up for what he had lost.

'Washed your arms off yet, Michael?' Eugenia quipped as she dumped another trayload beside him.

Michael was just about to say something smart and cutting back when he noticed how tired she looked. It had been a very busy night and Eugenia wasn't used to *real* work, only studying. But in spite of being obviously worn out, she hadn't slacked. Michael was grudgingly impressed, so he just smiled and said, 'No, not yet. You doin' OK?'

To his astonishment, Eugenia smiled back – a proper smile, not smart or smirky. 'To tell the truth, I'm only just keeping up,' she said. 'Don't know how you do it, Michael.'

'You'll get used to it. You've done good!'

Now they were both astonished. In all the years in school together, neither had ever given the other credit for anything.

Malady and Julietta went home before the last customers finished their meals. Eugenia bussed the final lot of dirty dishes to the kitchen and flopped down in a chair. 'I'm bushed!' she said. 'Do you do this every night, Michael?'

'Yep, most nights,' he replied without looking at her. 'And *I'm* not even saving for college.'

Eugenia looked at her feet. He could see she was embarrassed and he was immediately sorry.

'I mean, it's great – that you're saving for college—' he spluttered.

'I'm not,' Eugenia interrupted flatly. 'I'm saving for the rent. Mum lost her job.'

31

Before Michael could say any more, or even remember to close his mouth, she was gone, slamming the door into the alley with a bang. He had always thought of Eugenia's life as comfortable and easy; it was a shock to find that she had problems, just like he did.

Michael finished at the sink and went out into the restaurant to sweep the floor. The place was almost empty now. Just one customer was left at the bar – a big old guy in a T-shirt and jeans, wearing an expensive watch that said 'tourist' as clearly as if he'd had it written on his forehead. Michael swept round the guy's feet, hoping he'd take the hint and leave, but he just smiled and didn't move.

Mr Joseph was cashing up behind the bar. 'Have a juice while I tot up your wages, Mikey,' he said. 'Hey, I heard about poor Edison – and his boats,' he went on. 'Was yours smashed up with the rest?'

Michael nodded, and gulped down his juice.

'You got a record of what you paid on it?' Mr Joseph asked.

Michael didn't really want to talk about it,

especially with the tourist guy listening in, but he knew Mr Joseph was just trying to be kind. 'Mr Levi wrote it in a notebook,' he answered quietly. 'But the construction guys threw that in the harbour. It sank.' He was sure the tourist guy was leaning closer to hear.

Mr Joseph sighed and shook his head. 'How much you lose?'

'Three hundred and twenty-seven dollars and fifty-eight cents.'

Mr Joseph whistled through his teeth. 'What'll you do?'

'No good trying to get it back from New Marine Enterprises' – Michael shrugged – 'and Mr Levi didn't have any family I can ask. So I'll just have to start again.'

'That's too bad, Mikey,' said Mr Joseph. 'Anyway, here's your wages, plus a little bonus for helping out at short notice. You'll get your boat in the end, I'm sure.'

Michael smiled and thanked him, but his boat had never seemed quite so far away.

The streetlights made pools of yellowish brightness on the dark road as Michael left the Flying Fish. He walked fast. Rose Town was as safe late at night as it was in the day, but he was tired and wanted to get home. Tomorrow he'd be looking for at least one more job, so he'd have to be up early. He was thinking so hard of other places where he might work that it wasn't until he'd passed the last hotel on the Old Town road – the last place where anyone from out of town might stay – that Michael realized the tourist was behind him. Surely he wasn't following him? That only happened in spy movies. All the same, when he reached the coconut palms on the edge of the road by Cat's Paw Beach, Michael stepped behind one of their trunks to see what the guy would do.

The man stopped at once and peered into the darkness under the moonlit trees, clearly looking to see where Michael had gone. He was taller than Michael had thought. He wore a suit jacket over his T-shirt now, which gave him a sort of square, cut-out look, and the brim of his panama hat hid his face in shadow. But his voice when he spoke was deep and friendly.

'There's nothing to be afraid of, lad,' he said. 'I'd like to talk to you about your boat, is all . . .' He left the sentence trailing like a fishing line.

It was too much to resist. Michael came out from behind the tree. But he kept his distance: what normal person would follow you in the dark rather than speaking to you in a well-lit bar?

'How d'you know about my boat?' Michael asked, although he knew perfectly well; the man's ears had been all but flapping.

'Well, I couldn't help overhearing your conversation in the bar . . .'

Michael waited.

The man went on, a little uncomfortably, 'My name's Spargo. I work for New Marine Enterprises. I'm sorry about your boat and what happened to Mr Levi.'

The man's face emerged from shadow and caught the moonlight: a big, broad face, with deep lines around the mouth, and at the corners of the eyes. An old face – weathered, like a piece of driftwood left in the sea. Michael listened to his accent. It was English, a voice from the country that had swallowed up first his mother and then his father. But not English like the people on the radio Gran listened to. There was a curl in the man's 'r's, as if his voice had been warmed up and cooked on a wood fire.

'I was a young chap like yourself, once. On shore and champing to be on the sea in my own craft. I'd like to offer you a job and the use of a boat and fishing gear. My boss and I, we need someone who can handle a boat, who knows the waters round 'ere. Someone who knows how to be quiet – discreet, like. Of course, we'd refund the down payments you made to poor Mr Levi. What do you say?'

A boat *and* his down payments returned? It was almost irresistible.

The man sounded trustworthy, even kind, but asking for someone who could be 'quiet' was suspicious. *Quiet about what?* Michael wondered; he hung back and stayed silent.

'Well,' Spargo said with a low chuckle, 'that proves you have one of the qualities we're looking for. Like I said, we need someone who can be quiet.'

Michael still said nothing.

The man hesitated. 'You don't have to make a decision now. I'm staying at the Rathborne. Come and see me tomorrow morning maybe?'

He bent down and put a business card on the moonlit sand, then turned abruptly and walked away into the night.

Michael stood looking at the card for a while. The whole thing stank – creeping about in the dark wanting someone who could keep their mouth shut! But he was curious: he stepped forward, picked up the card and turned it over. He could just read the name on it in the thin moonlight. *Spargo* – no 'Mr' and no initials. Why didn't he have a proper name?

Michael let out a long-held breath. A boat and fishing gear – his dream, lying here in his hand in the form of little bit of white card. For a moment he wanted to run down the road after Spargo and say, *Yes, yes!* But then his father's voice, deep and low as it always used to be, came back to him once more: *Remember, Mikey, the bigger the bait, the bigger and sharper the hook.*

Yes, a piece of bait as big as his dream must have a very big, very sharp hook at its centre.

Michael sighed. He thought about poor Mr Levi, 'dropped dead on the spot'. Spargo *had* seemed sorry about him, but there was too much that was suspicious about the old Englishman. No, he would rather wash up a stack of dishes higher than the Rockies and sweep a continent of dirty floors than do a deal with people who could snatch some old guy's boats, wreck his shack and then creep around trying to make deals in the dark.

Yet as Michael walked away from the beach, he found he'd put the little white business card in his pocket.

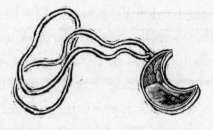

5

Sometimes Michael wished that Gran's house was right in town so his walk home late at night wasn't so long. Then he would be near school and his jobs and the quayside, and close enough to the power lines for them to have electricity in the house. But sometimes, like now, he loved the fact that it wasn't.

He breathed in the air, warm and spicy as a fruit cake. Frogs chirped, fireflies flashed their little green lights in the tops of Gran's trees, and there was no electric light to spoil the comfort of the dark. Down the hill, house lights and streetlights shone too brightly, and the few cars still on the road streaked the hillside with their headlights. Beyond the town was the greater darkness of the ocean, and tonight, far, far out to sea, a storm, with lightning flickering but too distant for thunder. From inside the house came the sound of his gran snoring gently like a big cat purring.

Michael lay on a blanket on the veranda to be close to the night. He would save the money for another boat. Tomorrow he would find *more* work to help him do it. He didn't need New Marine Enterprises or Spargo. Michael shut his eyes, and the sea dreams rushed in as they always did . . .

. . . *Michael and Samuel are far enough from shore for the island to be a tall fin, stretching along the eastern horizon. They know there are other boats somewhere out on the ocean, but it feels as if theirs is the only one. A still, blue day, with a swell soft as breathing; the boat moving up and then down in a sleepy rhythm. It is their last day at sea together, although Michael doesn't know it.*

They sit opposite each other, baiting their hooks with

40

chunks of ballyhoo, ready for a catch of bonito or jacks. They are happily silent for a long while; then his father speaks.

'When my great-grandfather was a boy,' Samuel says, his voice a soft, sweet growl, 'there would have been whales out here, right underneath our keel. Sperm whales, with their big square heads swimmin' around in two thousand feet of water. Just think of the mysteries they'd see down there, Michael, at the very bottom of the sea!'

And Michael feels the long column of blue water that stretches down and down and down underneath their boat, right beneath their feet at this very moment, and all the life it might contain. It's as if his father's soft, dark voice is reaching down there, taking Michael with it.

'My grandpa told me that there's a place – a place where the water runs deep enough to lose the highest mountain. That's where the whales come. So many you can walk on their backs.'

Michael can see it! This dark blue window of sea where whales crowd to the surface as easy as the bubbles in a glass of lemonade. His heart drinks in this image that his father created, not sure if it's made up, or real, or something in between.

Samuel goes on, 'And he told me that this is half of what you need to know to get there.'

From under his sun-faded shirt he pulls out a sliver of silver no bigger than his thumbnail, like a tiny shard of moonlight, threaded on a piece of string. He slips the string over Michael's head, and says, 'There – see? It's the head of one of those whales that used to swim right here.'

Michael runs his finger over the shape. There are words there too, but he's only just started school, so his father reads them for him, and Michael whispers after him, 'When Peter hides the Devil and . . .'

The words feel weighty and important, and Michael finds his eyes pricking with tears as he says them, though he's not sure why.

'Grandpa said it was a secret, son,' Samuel says with a big smile. 'It's our secret now!'

Michael nods, and it feels like their two hearts are beating at the same time—

'Davis! Davis!' Gran was shaking him awake, her eyes wild and her hair unbraided in a mad halo around her head. 'This storm's lifted the corner off the roof again,' she yelled. 'You need to go inside and watch your baby brother!'

Rain was hitting the roof like handfuls of gravel, and wind tugged at the edges of the tin sheets, strong as a man's arm. Lightning stunned the air into electric brightness, showing Gran's frightened face in terrifying clarity, then exploding the sky above their little house with a crack that banished all sense. The sudden noise and light scrambled Michael's brain, and for a moment he was limp as a doll in Gran's grasp.

He came to his senses, and flicked on the torch he kept by his bed for emergencies. Gran was dragging a raincoat on over her nightie, and she had a hammer in her hand.

'Now you stay here, Davis, and watch Samuel while Mummy goes on the roof and gets it all safe!' she said, trying to sound calm, even though it was clear she wasn't. She looked smaller and frailer than ever.

Michael knew exactly what Gran planned to do: climb up the little ladder on the wall at the back of the house to nail down the corner of the tin roof. He'd heard how she'd climbed up there in a storm and nailed it down once before, but that was more than thirty years ago. Somehow in Gran's mind it *was* that night long ago, when a hurricane had come and blown the island flat. She'd been a young woman then, raising her boys, Davis and Samuel, alone.

Michael looked at her and knew that he had to find a way to keep her off the roof. It was no good telling her that he wasn't her son, but her grandson, and that she was way too old to be crawling about on a rooftop in a gale. The only way was to go along with her in some way. He had never talked back to his gran, but he squared up to her now. He drew himself up tall and tried to look as manly as he could, pretending to be his own grandfather.

'Are you crazy, woman?' he said roughly. 'Can't you tell your own husband from your son? It's me, Ivor! No *way* are you goin' on that roof. Gimme that hammer!'

He snatched it from her and held out his hand for the nails. Quiet as a lamb, she gave them to him. The look on her face made his heart turn over, but it couldn't be helped.

Outside, the rain was coming down like spite. The wind threw it so it stung his skin. The little wooden ladder up to the roof was green with mould and slippery, and the wind made it rattle and shake horribly as he climbed. Michael crawled over the roof to the corner where the metal was loose and bouncing up and down in the gale; another ten minutes and the whole roof would have been flying over Rose Town, leaving Gran's little home open to the storm. He held the torch in his mouth, and shook his head to clear his eyes of the streaming water. Then he hammered the nails into place – one, two, three, four, five – until the roof was secure. Then he crept back across the roof, down the rickety ladder and went back inside.

He almost fell over Gran's body. She was slumped by the back door in a heap. For a terrible moment he thought she was dead, but then she gave a little moan and he knew she wasn't. The torch fell, smashed on the floor and went out. Michael froze in stupid indecision. Should he light the lamp so he could see properly to help her, or move her first? At last he lit the lamp with shaking hands, and half lifted, half dragged her to her bed.

She held a hand to her chest and groaned, then opened her left eye and spoke. Her voice was faint and her words slurred, but she was at least back in the real world of here and now.

'I know what you did.' She chuckled weakly. 'Got me to think you were my own Ivor.'

'Couldn't let you go out on that roof, Gran.'

'Don't you play that trick on me again, Michael.'

'OK, Gran. OK.'

* * *

Michael walked down the white hospital corridor. Gran was safe, with doctors and nurses to look after her. One of the nurses, an enormous lady with fancy blue-rimmed glasses who told him her name was Sister Taylor, explained what was wrong with Gran. She'd had a heart attack. Her heart had actually stopped for a moment and she could have died. She wasn't out of danger and she would need to be in hospital for a long while. It was going to cost a *lot* of money.

Sister Taylor was quite kind behind her scary glasses; she asked how old Michael was. He didn't want to be bundled off and cared for by strangers, because then who was going to earn the money to pay for Gran to get better? So he added on a few years – it was an easy lie to tell: he was tall for his age, and suddenly, with the worry and responsibility falling on his shoulders, he *felt* older. *Much* older. He hoped that he wouldn't be found out.

He told Sister Taylor that his dad would be arriving from England any day. His father had plenty of money, he said, he would pay for everything. For now, at least, she believed him, so he had time to come up with a plan.

The big doors swung open and let him out into the sunny morning. Michael stood on the pavement, feeling washed out. He pulled the business card out of his pocket.

SPARGO

MARINE ENTREPRENEUR

DEPUTY DIRECTOR, NEW MARINE ENTERPRISES

There was an address in a place Michael had never heard of, and a string of long telephone numbers. *Marine Entrepreneur* – what did *that* mean? Gran said that anyone who had to come up with a fancy name for what they did was probably up to no good. Michael guessed she was right. Why would someone want a boatman who 'knows how to be quiet'? There were no good reasons that Michael could think of. His father's warning about bait and hooks echoed in his mind again.

But he had no choice now. It wasn't about his dreams, or about chasing some story. This was *survival*. Washing dishes and sweeping floors wouldn't pay enough, but fishing just might, and the down payment he'd made to Levi would make a start on Gran's hospital bills. He couldn't afford to turn up his nose at Spargo's offer, however suspicious the old man seemed. Mr Levi had probably had a weak heart all along, Michael told himself.

St Mary's church clock chimed the hour. Nine o'clock. Just time to walk down to the Rathborne, the poshest tourist hotel in town, before they finished serving breakfast.

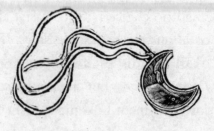

6

The Rathborne Hotel announced its name in gold letters over the entrance. There were palms in pots, an old cannon polished to a shine and a doorman in uniform. Michael waited until the doorman was helping some tourists into a taxi, and dodged inside.

The whale skeleton that had once stood in the reception area had been replaced with shiny leather sofas. It all looked expensive. To his great relief, Marlee was on reception. She had her hair and nails done at Gifted Hands almost every Tuesday afternoon, and Michael had chatted to her a few times.

'What you doin' in here?' she hissed. 'You wanna get me into trouble?'

He put the business card on the desk in front of her. 'I've got an appointment with Mr Spargo.'

Marlee's eyes opened wide and her carefully drawn eyebrows shot upwards. 'You *have*?'

She didn't look as if she believed him for a moment, but when she ended the call to Mr Spargo's room, her eyebrows were even further up her forehead.

'He says he'll meet you here in five minutes.' Marlee shook her head in disbelief. 'You are something else, Michael Fontaine. One minute you're sweeping up in a hair salon, and the next you're having a *meeting* with the guy who says he's gonna make Rose Town the busiest seaport in the Caribbean. *We* only found out who he was when the *Gazette* came out this morning.' She pushed the latest copy of the *Rose Town Gazette* towards him. 'You can read it while you wait.'

Michael perched on the edge of one of the

sofas as if he were sitting on red-hot rocks. The lobby was twice as big as the whole of his grandmother's house. Everything in it was new and polished. There was a huge mirror on the wall opposite him; he avoided looking in it. He didn't want to see quite how scruffy and out of place he seemed in this sleek setting, and concentrated on the newspaper Marlee had given him instead.

Spargo was on the front cover. He recognized the crumpled jacket and pale hat, the big square body; the broad, smiling face, eyes sparkling in a nest of crow's feet. He looked nicer in the picture than he had seemed in real life, Michael thought. Spargo was shaking hands with the mayor, and smiling as if smiling were something he knew all about and could offer you lessons in.

ROSE TOWN TRANSFORMATION! the headline over the photograph said. Michael read on.

Spargo, right-hand man to the mysterious international business magnate known only as 'JJ' who heads up New Marine Enterprises, or

NME, has pledged to make Rose Town great again. The old quay will become a Marine Exhibition Centre, with a very, very special exhibit at its heart.

'I can't give you any details yet,' Mr Spargo told the Gazette, 'but I can promise that once the Rose Town Marine Centre opens its doors, people will come from all over the world to see what it holds!'

The fish market too will get a complete makeover, with state-of-the-art refrigeration and packaging facilities.

'I grew up in a Cornish village that depended on the sea,' Mr Spargo says, 'so I know about places like Rose Town. In a few weeks – perhaps as soon as Carnival time – thousands of tons of marine products will be packed and frozen at the new fish market and sent all over the world. Tourists will flock to the Marine Exhibition Centre. This will bring jobs and prosperity to the whole island of Liberty!'

As a gesture of goodwill, the NME will build

a new road across the island, and a new high school for Rose Town.

'We are incredibly fortunate that NME has chosen to invest in the future of Rose Town,' said Mayor Lennox Shillingford. 'Everyone is very excited about this chance to put Rose Town back on the world map.'

Michael stared at the photograph of the beaming mayor and the two men's clasped hands. A new road, a new school and a new fish market. *Huh!* Michael thought. *No wonder Mr Levi wasn't mentioned anywhere!*

There was no time to wonder about anything else, such as why JJ was 'mysterious' or what would be so 'special' about the plans for the Marine Exhibition Centre, because Spargo was standing in front of him.

'Good to see you, Michael!' he said, smiling the same wide, white-toothed smile he had in the photograph. In daylight Michael could see that Spargo was *really* old – but not worn-out old, like

Gran was. He looked as if his years had made him stronger and tougher, as if he could carry an elephant up all Liberty's mountains without breaking a sweat.

Michael stood up. He took the man's outstretched hand and greeted him politely. 'Morning, Mr Spargo.' Spargo's hand was like a bear's paw, huge and strong.

'Ah, glad you can speak then, lad! But none of that Mister nonsense. I been plain Spargo all me life and I ain't changing now!'

Spargo's deep laugh seemed to command you to join in; reluctantly, Michael smiled back.

'So do you agree to my offer?'

The old man leaned closer to Michael and spoke quietly, but still the question sounded like a challenge, a mixture of being asked to fight *and* dance. He could already tell that saying 'no' to Spargo would be hard; dangerous even.

Michael nodded. 'Yes. I agree,' he said, trying to sound as grown up and serious as possible.

Spargo straightened up. He moved slowly and

deliberately, yet seemed to fizz with energy. 'Well, no time like the present. C'mon, lad.'

He strode across the hotel foyer, and Michael rushed after him.

A car was waiting outside. It had special windows that you couldn't see in from the outside, but once inside, you could see a shaded version of the world. It had deep leather seats and it was air-conditioned too, so that Michael stepped from the already baking heat of a Rose Town morning into a chill like the inside of a fridge. Spargo leaned forward to say something in Spanish to the driver, then sat back, tapping messages into his phone. Almost no one in Liberty had a phone. Gran used to say that the mobile phone mast that stood on the hill outside Rose Town must be 'the loneliest thing on the island 'cos nobody talks to it'. Mayor Lennox said it was 'moving Rose Town into the future'. And here was the future, sitting larger than life in his own air-conditioned limo!

It was delicious to ride in the cool car. Michael watched the town slipping by outside. At the junction of the Bath Road, just before it crossed the bridge out of town, they passed Mrs Thomson's car parked outside the bakery. Eugenia was in the passenger seat. Michael wasn't sure if he wished the windows of the limo were not shaded, so that Eugenia could see him with Spargo, or glad that they were, so she wouldn't.

The boat was the only craft tied up at the private marina of a half-built hotel called the Golden Cove, which stood at the end of a long track, about five miles out of Rose Town. She was beautiful – not new, but with a fresh coat of paint, green outside and yellow in, and with *two* outboards, so if one went wrong you could still get home. She was a good size, yet still small enough for Michael to handle alone. There was a box of fishing gear too, a couple of sturdy handlines, hooks, a bait box and a gaff.

Michael jumped down into the stern and felt himself glowing with happiness and excitement in spite of his misgivings. Spargo looked down on him from the jetty, his hat in one hand, the other on his hip.

'All yours, Michael!' he exclaimed. 'I must say, you look pretty comfortable there! Reminds me of me own first boat when I was nipper. *That's* a fair old time ago, I can tell you.'

Spargo beamed, but his jolly smile seemed forced, and Michael found himself wondering if this big tough man could ever have been a little child, a 'nipper'. But still, he wanted to impress Spargo and make sure that the boat would be his.

'I was out in my father's boat all the time,' he told the old man.

'Yes,' Spargo replied. 'I heard about that.'

How had he 'heard'? Spargo saw the questioning look on Michael's face. 'Your employer, Mr Joseph, told me about you and your da out in the boat,' he said quickly, stretching out a hand to help Michael out of the boat. 'Come inside, lad. We need to talk business.'

Michael took the hand, and the man pulled

him effortlessly up onto the jetty. He followed Spargo inside the unfinished hotel. The bar was all concrete and bare wires, but it was shady and relatively quiet, although sounds of drilling and hammering came from other parts of the building. Work was going on, even though it was the weekend. They sat down on two rickety folding chairs on either side of a packing case.

'OK, so let's get to business.'

Spargo was still smiling, but all the time Michael was aware of something colder underneath, as if there were another, quite different sort of face behind the one that Spargo showed him. But this was business, so Michael pushed his unease aside.

'First, it's important that no one knows where you got the boat,' Spargo said. 'I don't care what you say, just so long as it isn't anything to do with NME, OK?'

His blue eyes looked across the packing case at Michael like a pair of lasers. Michael didn't like lying, and he wondered why such secrecy was necessary . . . But standing in the boat had felt so good.

He took a deep breath and nodded. 'That's fine.'

'Good!' Spargo beamed. 'Second, this boat is for your use only. No crew! Right?'

Two people in a boat was safer than one; that way you had someone to haul you back if you fell overboard, but plenty of fishermen went out alone. In any case, Michael had always imagined having his boat to himself, so he nodded again.

'Now we're cooking!' Spargo rubbed his big hands together like a child who'd been promised a treat. 'So you can use the boat, sell your catch, *and* we'll pay you for what *we* need you to do . . .'

It was great offer . . . too good to be true. Samuel's voice whispered in Michael's ear, *Where's the hook?* What would Spargo want in return for all these odd promises? Something illegal? Something bad? Was it too late to walk away? Michael's heart beat in his throat as Spargo leaned forward over the rickety little table, and lowered his voice.

'OK, Michael, so far so good, eh? What I'm about to tell you is strictly, *strictly* just between us – a secret.'

Michael swallowed.

Spargo went on, 'When this hotel is completed, JJ and I want to run boat trips for tourists – dolphin watching, you know?'

Michael did. It was one of the things he and his father had spoken of. They had often seen dolphins when they were out in the fishing boat.

'Obviously we don't want any competition from other hotels,' Spargo explained. 'Your job is to survey the entire west coast of the island and keep a record of where and when you see dolphins. I gather you've done something similar in the past with your da, eh? Course, you can fish to make some extra cash and cover your real task, but you'll be our spy at sea!'

Michael almost laughed out loud with relief. Nothing illegal – just dolphin spotting! But Spargo wasn't finished.

'We also want to know where *whales* can be

found in these waters.' He said the word in a funny way, more like 'wu-hales' – slowly, as if he didn't want the word to get away from his mouth. His eyes glittered as he spoke, and a steel edge slipped into his voice. He was like a miser grasping at a precious jewel.

Michael's hand wanted to reach for the medallion under his T-shirt, but he didn't let it. Spargo couldn't possibly know about the whale charm. If he *really* knew anything about the island, then he'd know that no one had seen a whale for decades. It was just wishful thinking, and if the old man wanted to pay Michael to chase something that wasn't there, that was *fine*.

Spargo gave him a compass, a watch and a notebook. 'Every sighting of a dolphin or *wu-hale* goes in here,' he said, tapping the hard cover of the book. 'Every one with a date, time and position. Right?'

Michael nodded. He put the watch on his wrist; it was a digital one with lots of buttons and dials. Instantly he felt more grown up and important.

'So then we can mark the sightings on a chart,' Spargo added, 'and find the best places to send the tourists when the new hotel opens – that way we'll be ahead of the competition. One day, Michael, there could be a job for you as skipper of a dolphin-watching boat. What do you say to that?'

Michael had to remember to close his mouth and then try not to grin like an idiot. 'I'd like that very much, Spargo,' he said, as soberly as he could manage.

Michael was to go out in the boat every day that conditions allowed. This meant giving up on school.

'Shouldn't think you're any more of a scholar than I was, eh, lad?' Spargo said.

He was right. Michael had never been a good student, and he already knew he'd have to work, not study, to pay Gran's hospital bills. That was fine. He was tall enough to pass for three or four years older than he was, and plenty of boys that age were working on boats and construction sites rather than staying on at school. Eugenia would have no one to scold there any more, but apart from that, no one would miss him.

'So, I'll just recap, shall I?' Spargo sat back in his chair, as if he were about to tell a joke or drink a beer. 'One: you keep the boat's ownership quiet. Two: you don't take crew. And, *most important of all*, three: you record every dolphin and *wu-hale* sighting you make. OK?'

Michael nodded.

The laser-blue eyes glinted coldly in their deep creases. 'We may not meet for a while now,' Spargo said. 'Better, in fact, if we aren't seen together. But you've given your word and I'll trust you to keep it.'

He took Michael's hand in his big paw. 'We'll shake on it, then, man to man, eh?'

Even though Michael didn't trust him entirely, it felt good to be spoken to like a grown man. He stopped smiling and squared his shoulders. Yes, there were things about this deal he didn't like, but there were others he liked very much, such as the prospect of one day being the skipper of a dolphin-watching boat! Wasn't Gran always saying, *Life is not perfect. Sweet always comes with a little salty?*

Maybe there was a hook inside this bait, but for now Michael decided it was best not to look for it.

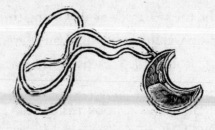

7

Spargo headed back into town, but Michael couldn't wait to get out on the sea. As he had nothing to do until Gran's visiting hours began in the evening, he decided to start at once and take the boat out for her first voyage. Spargo didn't want a name painted on the side, but Michael named her in his head anyway: the *Louisa May*, after his gran.

It was a fine, calm day, a good day for getting used to a new boat and a new engine. He was excited, but worried that, after so long, there might be important things he'd forgotten. But from the moment he cast off, everything about the boat – the mooring rope, the tiller, the tone of the engine, the slap of the water on her hull – instantly felt as much a part of him as his own limbs. He felt sharp and alert, a different person from the boy who sat crammed behind a desk in school all day, being scolded by Eugenia Thomson and dreaming of escape. He felt his whole spirit unfold and run free over the water.

He pointed the boat's nose straight out. The singing surface of the ocean and the shimmering line of the horizon filled his heart. All the dishes he had washed, the floors he had swept, the worry about Gran and her hospital bills – all of it simply fell away. At last, at long, long last, he was back where he belonged!

A mile out from shore Michael idled the engine and baited his lines the way his father had taught him. Then he motored gently a short way to trawl the hooks through the water and show them to any fish that might be around, before turning off the engine and waiting.

Michael looked around and breathed deep.

This was what he had longed for – real sea, away from the noise of people and surf. Trucks on the coast road were just silent specks of movement, and all the buildings at Golden Cove had melted into the backdrop of green. The surface stretched out from him in all directions, connected to every other place that the ocean touched, while he floated here, tiny as a leaf.

He pulled out the compass that Spargo had given him and practised taking bearings. Lapoulet Head was at 70 degrees and Pointe Maron at 109. The point where those two lines crossed was where he was. This was another thing he'd learned from his dad, although when they were out on the boat together, they hardly ever used a compass. They navigated by eye, using landmarks you could see out on the ocean. Michael remembered Samuel saying, *When you're in line with Calibishy church, about a mile out, that's a good spot for fishing. Halfway between Pointe Caribi and Anse Matoo is a reef; steer clear of that or you'll put a hole in the boat.*

Samuel had made him learn the names of the mountains that stood along the island's spine. Their shapes were clear against the sky, trailing little bits of cloud – and steam where their hot, volcanic breath seeped into the air. *They're your friend, son; they'll always guide you home.*

Michael said their names over in his head: Morne Matin and Morne Marie to the south, Morne Liberty, and the highest, Morne Pierre, in the north. A course set to Morne Matin would get you home to Rose Town. One set to Morne Marie would take you to Soubière, the little town where Gran had been born. There was a reef in the mouth of the bay, but there was a sure way to avoid it: *When Pitoo Head hides Soubière church,* Samuel had told him, *steer hard starboard.*

Michael said the words over again: *When Pitoo Head hides Soubière church . . .* They reminded him of the mysterious words on his medallion.

When Peter hides the Devil . . .

Perhaps the words weren't a riddle at all, but simply directions; the way to navigate a course,

69

like the way around the Soubière reef? The old whalers had navigated the same way he and his dad did, lining up features on the land to find their way about at sea. Wasn't Pierre another name for Peter? Morne Pierre could be Peter in the riddle! Michael's heart gave a jump. For a moment he felt quite excited – but what would Morne Pierre *hide* that was named after a Devil? He couldn't think of a single headland, mountain, beach or bay with *Devil* in its name.

No. *No, no, no!* It was *crazy.* The words on the medallion came from superstitious old whalers, he told himself; it was only a *story,* just as Dad said it was.

Besides, the fish were biting. Michael concentrated hard on hauling jacks as big as silver dinner plates into the boat, until his arms ached and his hands were cut raw by the line.

As the sun began to sag towards the west, Michael headed home. A school of dolphins surfaced fifty metres from his bow. The low light on the calm water caught the vapour of their spouts, turning them to little puffs of gold. Their round foreheads broke the surface, and the sharp sickle curve of their dorsal fins followed, slicing the water into slivers of light. They were too small to be bottle-nosed dolphins and too big to be spinners. Michael counted ten, twelve, sixteen; there might be twice as many under the surface each time he saw them blow. They swam closer, and he saw the spots freckling their skins, confirming that they were spotted dolphins. He speeded up in the hope that they might bow-ride, but they were heading out to sea, ready for a night's hunting in deeper waters, and they disappeared like a dream. A few moments later he glimpsed their fins cutting the surface far off; it was always amazing to see how fast dolphins could swim.

It was the first time since his dad left that Michael had been so close to dolphins. A bubble of longing to share this moment with Samuel rose up, but he pushed it down; this was business now. He took a bearing – on Pointe Maron, Soulant

Head, and a third on the needle-like summit of Morne Matin, to be extra sure – and wrote it down with the date and time next to SPOTTED DOLPHIN in the log book Spargo had given him. It was a fine first day's work.

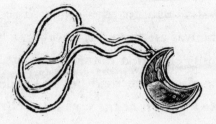

8

Inside a week Michael had established a new routine for himself. He had decided for the time being to keep the boat moored at Golden Cove. That way it was easy to say that the boat wasn't his, or not to mention it at all. He could still get back into town at the end of the day in time to visit Gran.

He left Rose Town before dawn on the first minibus running up the coast towards Northport. That early, there were no school kids around, and nobody else he knew to ask awkward questions. He wore an old checked shirt of his father's and pulled a baseball cap down low on his forehead.

That was enough for the other passengers to assume he was an apprentice working on one of the building sites that dotted the coast. He got off at the rise in the road before Golden Cove and walked the rest of the way, down the mile of dirt track to the half-built hotel. He was aboard the *Louisa May* and casting off just as it got light, before the construction workers had wiped the sleep out of their eyes.

Her two outboards were small engines and her hull was broad and homely. She was a steady fishing platform, but no speedboat, making his progress slow. Each day he surveyed a different bit of coast, looking out for dolphins and leaving time for fishing in the best spots his father had showed him.

Michael revelled in the new rhythm of his days and the moods of the ocean: the dawn coming up from the far side of the island and the dreamy stillness of the water close to shore; the hot mid-days, two miles out, with the breeze picking up and the water choppy and deep blue; and the sweetness of dusk, coming back to land, and the green smell of trees.

It was exciting to bait his own hooks and haul them in, heavy and wriggling with fish. Carrying his catch from the *Louisa May* gave him the deepest sense of pleasure. Selling them proved easier than he'd imagined because, from the first time he returned to the jetty with fish, it was clear that the construction workers would buy all he could catch. They never left the site and seemed very pleased to have a ready supply of fresh fish. They spoke only Spanish, but the sign language bargaining worked pretty well. They agreed that every night he'd put the fish in the big fridge in the unfinished kitchen, and they would leave his money in a biscuit tin on top. This was also where Michael had to leave his weekly report of dolphin sightings for Spargo, and where Spargo left his wages. At the end of the first week the repayment of Michael's boat money had also been in the tin. He'd returned to town with more cash in his pocket than he'd ever seen in his life.

His daytime life of the boat and sea felt wonderful, free and full of light. But at the end of every day, as dusk fell and he got the bus back to Rose Town, all the worries of life on land came and settled on his heart like shadows: what if Gran didn't get better? The three hundred dollars from Michael's boat down payment had taken care of the first hospital bill, but there would be more – and what would happen if he couldn't pay? *Nobody's gonna look out for you and me, my boy, so we just got to do it for our own selves*, Gran had always said, except that now it wasn't him and Gran; it was just him all alone.

He'd written to his father telling him about Gran's illness and asking him to come home, but he'd lost hope even before he posted it: Samuel had never replied before – the address was surely years out of date. The letter would never find him.

So at the end of every day Michael trudged into the hospital with a heavy heart and sat at his gran's bedside. For the first few evenings she hadn't even opened her eyes. The nurses said she was really sick, but told him not to worry. He thought they were crazy: if she was ill, how was he supposed *not* to worry? Perhaps she was too old and too tired to ever be well again.

But then, one evening, as he sat beside her, her eyes flew open, and her hand, which had been limp as a wet leaf, gripped his tightly. 'I hope you aren't missing your studies to be here,' she breathed.

Michael could barely speak for smiling, but he didn't want to let on that his studies were over.

'No, Gran. School finished hours ago. It's seven thirty.' That at least was true. He wanted to tell her about the boat. How he was earning money and behaving like a grown man. But he knew she would only worry.

'You look different,' she whispered, narrowing her bright eyes and looking at him keenly. 'You eating properly?'

'Lots of fresh fish, Gran,' he answered. 'I think I'm getting taller!'

She giggled. Michael's height was always a

source of pleasure to her. She sighed and slipped straight back to sleep with a smile on her face. Hope welled up in Michael's heart: she would get better, and he would pay off all their debts when he was skipper of a big dolphin-watching boat.

That night, when Michael walked into the kitchen of the Flying Fish, his relief must have shown on his face.

'So,' said Eugenia, dumping the first load of dirty dishes down by the sink, 'your gran's a bit better.'

'Yeah!' Michael beamed. 'She spoke to me. Wanted to know if I was eating properly!'

'And are you?' He could tell Eugenia was ready to waggle her finger at him. But it didn't irritate him any more. Even when she'd given him a hard time over quitting school he hadn't been angry. Somehow, these days they understood each other better. But he rolled his eyes at her now in mock anger, just to make her laugh, and she punched him on the arm.

'Well, I've got some good news too,' Eugenia said. 'Mum's got a new job at the university. Secretary to some scientist from Japan. So we won't get kicked out of our house!'

Michael smiled and then immediately frowned. 'Does that mean you'll stop working here?'

Eugenia flicked the end of her tea towel at him. 'Certainly not!' she quipped. 'Who knows what you'd get up to, Michael Fontaine, if I wasn't here to watch over you!'

He wanted to tell her what he *was* getting up to . . . about the *Louisa May*, the fishing, and how he was going to be skipper of Liberty's first dolphin-watching boat. But he knew Eugenia would ask all sorts of questions about Spargo that he didn't want to answer.

The relief about Gran carried him through an extra-long shift at the Flying Fish, but as he walked home past Cat's Paw, a wave of tiredness hit him like a train, and he had to sit down with his back against a tree. The sea sighed up the beach and stars danced on the water. So-So stepped out of the shadows. He was dressed in a robe made of knotted string and strips of fabric, and wore tin foil on his head like a crown.

'My star brother!' he exclaimed. 'I have not seen you this long time. Where you been?'

'Been working – on a boat,' Michael said quickly. 'Some guy in Northport, he got sick, so he's letting me use his boat.'

'Oh yeah?' So-So's voice was light as a breeze, but Michael could tell he saw through the lie at once. So-So sat down in front of him and placed his big hand right in the middle of Michael's chest. Even in the dark, Michael could see the slow burn inside So-So's eyes as they looked into his face.

'A weight of trouble and a burden of secrets sits on your heart,' he said, shaking his head.

'No, So-So,' Michael replied irritably. 'I'm *fine*. Just working hard, is all. I need to go home and sleep.' He pushed his old friend's hand away and got up.

'I worry for you, brother star,' So-So said sadly.

'You have false friends with powerful lies. You may not tell me, but still I know. Beware!'

So-So's foil crown clattered a little and caught the moonlight as Michael walked away.

On land, Michael's life felt like the dark time that was held between dusk and dawn. But back at sea in the morning he was in the light again, all shadows and worries burned away as the sun rose. The moment he jumped aboard his boat it was as if he was stepping into a different skin, living a different life. It was a relief to untie the boat from her mooring and leave the still sleeping island behind.

Memories of Samuel came flooding back, so that sometimes Michael felt that if he looked up quickly enough, he'd see his dad sitting by the tiller. He could almost hear his voice, telling him how to bait hooks, find the best spot for fish or tell one kind of dolphin from another.

The big grey ones, now, they're the bottle-noses. They like jumping and doing tricks; the spotted ones, though, not so much. But those little skinny ones – the ones you see in a big, big gang – they like jumping! Spinners, they are, 'cos they spin like a top, nose to tail.

Out in the boat with his father they'd seen dolphins, but not that often. Now there was hardly a day when Michael didn't see them. It was as if he were tuned into their presence, as if his senses were growing sharper.

And with every dolphin he saw, it was his father's voice that reminded him that perhaps there was more to be discovered in these waters.

There's a place where the water runs deep enough to lose the highest mountain. That's where the whales come. So many you can walk on their backs.

Just supposing there *were* still whales in these waters and the medallion really *did* hold the secret to finding them . . . ? If Michael could find them and show them to Spargo, then that job of skipper would surely be his. But if *the place where the whales come* was real and not a story, then was it also a real secret? His father's voice had something to say about that too, of course. *My daddy said it was a secret, son. It's our secret now!*

How could he reveal to Spargo, a man he didn't even trust, the one secret his father had left him to keep? Michael pushed these questions down under the surface like a float. But again and again they bobbed up, and wouldn't be ignored.

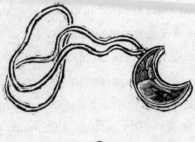

9

It was hot. Really hot. There wasn't the slightest breeze to cool the skin or make even a baby-finger crease on the surface of the sea. The *Louisa May* floated like a toy sitting on a glass table.

For the first time in over a week, Michael hadn't seen a dolphin all day. He was two miles offshore now, motoring along his daily survey course. The *Louisa May* pulled the reflection of the sky and the island into pleats behind her, and the *putt-putt* of her engine was lost in the big, quiet stillness of the afternoon.

Michael shut off the outboard and stopped. He leaned over the side to scoop up a bucket of seawater to cool himself, and looked down. Long fingers of sunlight slanted into the clear water, shifting slightly in arcs of radiating lines, and were swallowed up at last into the perfect blueness of the depths.

Water deep enough to lose the highest mountain . . .

Not that *deep just here*, Michael thought, *but perhaps two thousand feet.* Not enough to lose Morne Pierre, the highest mountain on the island, but deep enough to be beyond the reach of sunlight and warmth. This was where sperm whales had once lived; down there in utter darkness. The only light would have come in odd spots and dots from faintly glowing sea creatures. It was a world no human could visit or know. What would it be like down there? Michael wondered.

He poured the water over himself, savouring the delicious coolness.

Pppfffffwwwwraa! The sound came from close behind him, and made him spin round so fast he lost his balance and fell into the bottom of the boat.

Pppfffff – shorter and louder, even closer.

Michael picked himself up and looked over the gunwale.

A black shape, much, much bigger than the biggest dolphin, showed about five metres from the boat. It was like a polished rock. On its rounded side was a slit like a flattened S, bigger than a man's two clenched fists, with a raised lip around it. As Michael watched, astonished, not understanding what he was seeing, the lips pinched together, the hole closed, and the black shape sank rapidly beneath the sluicing water.

Now his brain had time to catch up with his racing heart.

A whale! Its dark head and blowhole! That's what he had seen.

Pppfffffwwwwraa!

Now it had surfaced on the other side of the boat. This second surfacing was hardly less shocking than the first, although Michael just managed to stay on his feet and cross the boat this time.

The whale was a little further away now, but

more of its body was thrust above the surface. Two, perhaps three metres of a giant, black oblong, smooth and rounded, stuck up out of the water. The blowhole was at the top; much lower, only visible above the waterline for a moment, was an eye. The rest of the body was a confused shadow under the surface, which had been ruffled by the whale's movement. It was hard to judge how big the creature was, but Michael thought its head must have been bigger than his whole boat.

A sound was coming from it. The whale was beaming it at him. A fast ticking, like a vast over-wound clock, but so powerful that Michael felt the clicks entering his body like a stream of bullets. He'd heard dolphins doing something like this. His father had said it was how they found their way around, deep down where there was no light. They made sounds and listened to the echoes to get a kind of picture.

The whale kept doing its clicking while it swam around the boat. Michael felt pinned to the spot, unable to do anything but cling to the side of his boat and follow the whale with all his attention.

The surface bent and buckled like molten glass, but he could see the whole of the submerged body as it swam on its side around the boat.

It was enormous. Two or three times the length of the *Louisa May*, and the strangest shape, quite unlike a dolphin. This creature seemed to be almost half head. And what a head! Square from the side, with the skinny little jaw, speckled white, slung underneath like a hinge. Head and body together were like a fat torpedo that tapered towards the huge tail, which beat up and down, slow, but full of grace and power.

Below the big expanse of head and above the paddle-shaped flipper was the eye. It sat in a moulded crease like a sort of naked eyebrow, which gave the whale an enquiring look. The white of the eye was clearly visible, with the dark iris sitting at the centre. Its gaze, like its clicks, was intense and full of energy as it looked right at him.

The clicks stopped abruptly, and the whale

began to swim around the boat the other way, showing Michael its other side: a mirror image, apart from four white parallel lines – scars perhaps – that marked the right side of its head.

Then, as suddenly as it had appeared, it turned its head downward. The triangular tail rose up like a strange sea-tree, breaking the surface of the water into a thousand reflecting fragments, then sliced downwards. Its beating left a backwash, a perfect circle of smooth water.

Michael breathed in and out carefully, still holding the boat so tightly his fingers hurt. He struggled shakily to the tiller and put the engine into gear to move over the exact spot where the whale had gone down. He stared over the side in wonder. Somewhere below his keel the whale was swimming down and down, into the dark of the deep. The water slapped blue against the underside of the boat and the engine puttered; the only other sound was the blood pumping in his ears.

PPPPPPFFFFFWWWWAAA!

It was louder than the bursting valve on a

pressure cooker, and even more of a shock than before, as Michael had been sure the creature had dived. But it had only gone down far enough to be invisible to him in the glint of the sun. It had bobbed up the moment his back was turned, at the stern of his boat.

Once again Michael could see the neat white lines scored along its head. It swam around the *Louisa May*, only just under a thin film of water, so Michael could clearly see the eye looking up at him, its expression searching and clever. He couldn't help feeling that the whale was laughing at him.

Once again it turned, upended and showed its splendid tail. It left behind another circle in the water as it submerged. Michael waited, looking over one side of the boat and then the other, but this time the whale reappeared more than a hundred metres away. It looked like a log lying on the surface, its back very straight and dark. For a moment he couldn't decide which end of the whale was its head. Then there was a puff of breath from its blowhole, a grey mist against the blue of the sea, and he had it: *there* was the squarish front of its head, and *there*, the knobbly dorsal fin. It was heading almost directly north-east. Without another thought Michael began to follow.

For an hour or more he kept directly behind the whale as it moved along at the surface. He watched the sea sluicing over the top of the head; it looked like a big water tank. From behind, it was clear that the blowhole was not in the middle of the creature's head but off to the left, in the extreme left-hand corner of the big 'tank'. The only other part of its body that was visible was its back, between the dorsal fin – not so much a fin as a hump – and the tail flukes. This was a dark, knobbly line that reminded him of the mountains along the top of the island, or a picture he had seen of a crocodile's tail.

In the bright, slanting light it was impossible to see down into the water, and after a while Michael found himself longing to see the whole of the whale once more – not just the small sections of it that showed dark and shiny, and a little confusing, above the surface. When it had approached the boat before, the engine had been quiet. Perhaps if he stayed where he was, it would come close again.

He shut off the outboard and waited, perfectly still on the glassy sea.

Up ahead, the whale had vanished. Michael scanned the ocean all around, shading his eyes with his hand and looking intently at the smooth sea around the *Louisa May*, which sat light as a floating leaf.

Nothing. No sign of a head or fluke or fin. Not even a skittering pack of flying fish, or a lone tropic bird, or the pebble-like head of a surfacing turtle.

Michael didn't hear or see what happened next; he felt it – a light scraping along the underside of the boat. It was the gentlest of touches that disguised an incredible strength, like being stroked by a giant's palm. Michael froze; the whale was right underneath the boat, holding the *Louisa May* on top of its flipper. He was completely in its power. It could lift the boat out of the water, or tip her over and smash her to bits. And yet he wasn't afraid. The whale was just holding itself under the boat, as if trying something out to see what it felt like.

Carefully, Michael leaned over to look: on the starboard side of the boat lay the whale's tapering tail stock and the flukes; on the port side, the head with its scarred lines, lay like a piece of huge, dark wreckage. This close, Michael could see that big sections of skin had peeled off in straight lines, giving the whale's head a patchwork look in greys and blacks. And closest of all to the boat, only just submerged, was the whale's eye. Michael looked right into it, and the whale looked back. It was so very, very close. He leaned out further and further, stretching his hand slowly towards it. The whale didn't draw away. He reached down, until his fingertips touched the crease of skin that gave the whale a kind of eyebrow. It was cool and smooth, like a carved stone covered in a finely stretched coat of rubber.

And as his fingertips touched the whale, he looked into its eye. It was impossible to say what colour it was: dark but with rays of brightness. It was like a window into a whole galaxy, with stars and planets, comets and supernovae moving inside.

Effortlessly, as if movement and thought were the same thing, the whale submerged out of reach of Michael's hand. There was a last shushing sigh as the flipper caressed the boat one more time, and then they were separate again. Michael watched as the whale sank directly below him. Against the background of featureless blue that gave no clue to distance, the whale seemed to be shrinking. At last it hung suspended in the water, looking no longer than Michael's forearm: the grey cylinder of its head and body, then the tapering tail stock, and finally the lovely triangular tail. The whale turned its head away from the surface, and the tail beat with a slow, sad rhythm, propelling the creature down and down, until finally it was lost in the blue deep.

The setting sun made a path over the sea, bathing Michael in golden light. He felt as if he were lit up inside too. He had touched a whale and looked into its eye! Like a sleeper waking from a dream, he looked around, dazed.

He was much further north than he'd expected. The jagged outline of Cape Paradis, the most northerly point of the island, was within sight. He took some bearings and fixed his position with the compass. He lined up the top of Morne Pierre and then the rocks of Cape Paradis: where the two lines crossed, that was where the whale had dived.

Michael wrote in the log book: date, time, position, but where the words *sperm whale* should have been, he left a blank. The medallion with its silver whale rested cool on his skin, reminding him that, for now at least, the whale should remain his secret.

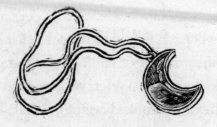

10

It was really too late for visiting hours by the time he got to the hospital, but Sister Taylor was just going off duty and she let him in to see Gran.

'She's a bit agitated tonight, Michael,' she said. 'She may ramble a bit.'

Gran's eyes weren't open but she wasn't sleeping. Her body was tense, and under their lids her eyes darted about. Her fingers danced on the sheet as if playing an invisible keyboard, and wouldn't lie still even when Michael took her hand.

'Gran?' he said softly. 'Gran? How are you feeling?'

To Michael's surprise, she snapped at him, but

without opening her eyes. 'Well, that's a foolish question, Samuel Fontaine!' she said. '*I'm* fine. *I'm* not the one going on a wild-goose chase to England! She's a wicked woman – she always was, and you're a *fool* to be going after her!'

Michael realized at once that Gran was talking about his mother.

'What's wicked about her, Ma?' he asked; Samuel always called Gran 'Ma'.

'You *know* what's wicked about her, Sam. Her family made servants of the likes of you and me, and they're still doing it. Don't go after her, Samuel! *Don't go!*'

Gran clutched his hand and opened her eyes at last. 'Oh!' she gasped. 'I was dreaming . . . Michael, it's *you!*' All the tension went out of her, like a puppet whose strings had been cut. She sank back into the bed and shut her eyes; this time she really *was* asleep.

Michael had never heard Gran or Samuel say so much about his mother, or anything at all about her family. Yet here was a glimpse of a bigger, darker history than he had ever imagined. It was like a reef lying invisible under the surface. He sat holding Gran's hand and feeling very alone, shut out of his own life, until the night nurse told him he had to leave.

It was raining, and everyone was indoors, out of the weather. The Flying Fish was closed on Monday nights, so Michael could go home and sleep. But without Gran, the house was empty and sad. He decided to go back to Golden Cove instead. The walk would take an hour or more; then he could sleep on the floor of the hotel and get an early start. He hunched his shoulders against the wet and stomped down the street.

Spargo's car was parked outside the Rathborne; as Michael passed, a woman got out. She was obviously hiding her face: she wore enormous sunglasses even though it was night time. A scarf covered her hair and part of her face. Even hidden behind all that, and the umbrella held by the doorman, Michael could tell that she was pretty, and quite young. Was she Spargo's daughter? Or even his wife? Rich old men often had pretty young wives, Michael knew.

'Welcome to the Rathborne, Miss JJ,' he heard the doorman say.

JJ? So the mysterious JJ, head of NME, wasn't a crusty old guy, as Michael had imagined! He stared after the woman as she disappeared into the brightness of the hotel lobby: it was odd, but there was something familiar about her. Must be the sunglasses, he told himself, that made her look like a movie star trying not to be noticed! Spargo was probably in the car, waiting for Michael to pass, so they wouldn't be seen together again. It seemed like a lot of secrecy just to keep the location of a few dolphins quiet. Michael shrugged and headed off into the rain.

Twenty minutes later, when he was clear of the last houses in Rose Town and walking along a dark section of coast road, Spargo's car drew alongside.

'Get in, Michael!' Spargo ordered. 'You're soaked, lad. What are you up to?'

'Going to get an early start!' Michael replied. He wanted to ask about 'JJ', but before he could think of a polite way to do it, Spargo was scolding him:

'Early starts are all very well,' he grumbled, 'but *results* are what matter. What have you *found*?'

There was none of the usual cheery manner; Spargo's voice and expression were hard and searching, and there was a knife-edge glitter to his eyes. Michael knew what he wanted to hear: about the whale; but he wasn't going to get what he wanted.

'Lots of dolphins,' Michael told him enthusiastically. 'Three different kinds so far.'

'Hmmmm,' Spargo said, unimpressed. 'And is that *all*?'

He lowered his voice to a gravelly whisper, and leaned even closer, big and square and menacing. 'You know,' he growled, 'I have good information that there *are* whales – sperm whales – in these waters, and it would very, *very* good for your future if you were to find them. You understand?'

Spargo's voice was like a crowbar trying to lever Michael's mind open. It was hard to resist: he just nodded earnestly without saying a word, and was very glad that they had arrived at Golden Cove so he could get out of the car.

Just as it was drawing away, the window wound down and Spargo peered out. He'd put on a friendly smile. Perhaps he knew that he'd shown Michael too much of what lay beneath.

'I'll be busy with the building work in town now for a while,' he said, less gruffly. 'But remember, our plans depend on you, lad. Find those whales!'

Michael nodded, but when he lay down on the floor of the bar to sleep, his thoughts churned in uncomfortable circles. Telling Spargo about the whale might mean a job that would keep him and Gran in the future, but there was something about the old man and his glamorous boss that Michael found very suspicious.

He woke to find that the sky had cleared and the stars were blazing. There was the faintest hint of grey in the eastern sky over the island. Michael took a packet of cookies and a bottle of water from the builders' kitchen, stepped down into his boat and cast off.

The outboard left a trail of ghostly phosphorescence, marking Michael's course directly west from Golden Cove in faint green neon. In half an hour he would turn north, and by then it would be getting light.

There was a sudden dark flutter in the twilight, and a noddy tern came to rest on the *Louisa May*'s stern, almost at Michael's elbow. It shuffled its small webbed feet along to find a comfortable position, then tucked its head under its wing and went to sleep. The bird's trusting presence seemed like a good omen.

Fingers of sunlight began to fan out over the top of the island. The western horizon appeared, separating sea and sky and darkness from each other. The little tern woke, preened briefly, pulling the end of each wing through the narrow tweezers of its beak, and flew off.

As the *Louisa May* headed out to sea, long low swells moved through the water, like the breathing of a great animal. Michael washed his face with seawater to wake himself up, squared his shoulders and set his course. He told himself that he was simply going to continue with the survey; he wasn't looking for the whale. But although his head knew it was simpler not see the whale again, his heart felt differently; when he reached the spot where it had been, he couldn't help stopping to scan the sea again and again. There was nothing but a distant line of terns dipping into the surface, and the black zigzags of frigate birds high in the sky. Nothing disturbed the surface – not a spout, not a dorsal fin. Michael told himself he was feeling disappointed because he hadn't seen any dolphins, but he knew that wasn't true.

He settled down to fish and began to bait his hooks. Almost at once he felt rather than heard, *Sssshhhh.*

A whispering touch on the underside of the boat, no more than the lightest brush from a tangle of floating seaweed. But Michael knew at once what it was!

Ppppppppfffff!

The whale's spout exploded right under the *Louisa May*'s port side, and a huge black triangle poked above the water to starboard. The scraping against the hull grew more definite, until the *Louisa May* was being very slightly lifted, no longer floating in the water.

Cautiously, his heart racing, Michael leaned over the port side. There, once again, was the great square head with its four white scars. There was the eye – a dark universe staring up through the film of water.

But the whale didn't stay still. Its tail disappeared and it no longer scraped under the *Louisa May*. Its great rock of a head popped up right at her bow and emitted a long stream of mad, tick-tocking clicks. Fascinated, Michael moved towards it, feeling the clicks hitting his breastbone and resonating through his chest. The patchwork of rubbery skin was close enough to touch. He felt irresistibly drawn to it, and reached out, but at the last second the whale dipped below the surface as if pulled down by its tail. Michael looked into the water to see the whole length of the creature's body. But today the surface was a frustrating jumble of reflecting shards. Forgetting all caution, he leaned further and further out, holding on with just one hand and shading his eyes with the other.

Pþþþþþffffffff!

The whale came up at the stern. It hit the propeller with its head and the whole boat suddenly jolted, tipping Michael into the water.

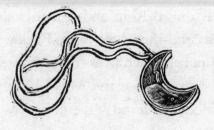

11

Michael immediately understood the danger he was in. He had to get back to the boat before the swells and the current made her drift out of reach. But before he could take a single stroke, the whale was between him and the *Louisa May*, so big and so close it was almost all he could see.

It hung at the surface, completely still, much more massive now that he was in the water with it. He felt tiny and completely vulnerable. Helpless. He remembered the whale teeth he had seen years ago in the Rathborne, set in the jaw of the skeleton, each one longer than his hand and wickedly pointed. What did sperm whales eat?

He remembered a picture in a book of a sperm whale and a huge squid. Perhaps he was a little squid-like himself, with his arms and legs poking out like tentacles. There was nothing he could do to defend himself; nothing but tread water and watch the *Louisa May* drifting further and further away.

The huge head moved forward, slowly and smoothly. The whale didn't seem like a creature that was about to attack. Yet instinctively, Michael reached out his hands to ward it off, and his palms slipped over its skin. It was the smoothest thing he had ever touched, like curved wet glass, but springy and warm rather than hard and cold. Not dead like glass, either, but singingly alive, as if a million tiny vibrations were happening under his hands. It was so intense a sensation that Michael gasped in surprise and snatched his hands away as if touching something red hot, but the whale kept coming, pushing him, slow and irresistible as a continent. Michael's hands slid apart and the whale moved into his arms like an embrace.

He was spread over the front of its snout like a starfish. Under the slippery skin, Michael sensed the vast workings of the mountainous body, the unimaginable strength and power. But this wasn't what astounded him; it was the creature's perfect control of its motion and its infinite, tender gentleness that left him breathless. He was not terrified at all but awed, overwhelmed.

The clicks began again, at point-blank range now, blasting into Michael's body. But only for a moment. The whale had got the information that it wanted. It tipped its head backwards, and now Michael was resting on the front of its upward pointing nose, precariously supported just above the surface. A little beyond where his right fingertips stretched, he felt a vibration as the breath approached the blowhole and then: *Pppffff!*

Carrying Michael like a wet rag doll, the whale turned through the water towards the *Louisa May*, balancing him carefully so he didn't slip. He didn't see the boat behind him, only felt the gentle buffet of his head against its gunwale as the whale

108

shoved him against the side with perfect precision. Instantly, Michael reached out, grabbed the edge of the boat and scrambled aboard, kicking against the slippery step of the whale's skin. He fell into the bottom of the boat, panting, then spun round to see where the whale was – but there was only the circle of flat water to show where its tail had pushed it down, back into its deep ocean world.

It felt as if the whale had deliberately tipped him out of the boat, out of his container, his wrapper, just to see what he was; and, having found out, put him back. Could that really be true? Michael looked down at his clothes: a slick of black whale skin, oily and fine like slime, coated his T-shirt and was lodged under his nails. Proving that he hadn't dreamed what had just happened.

Michael didn't bother pretending that he wasn't looking for the whale any more. The excitement of being with a real wild whale pushed his worries about Spargo to the back of his mind. For the rest of the morning and into the afternoon he searched up and down, in and out, within sight of Cape Paradis, but didn't see a single whale blow. But the moment he stopped searching, the whale simply appeared right beside the boat, as if it had been waiting for him to keep still!

It was so close to the *Louisa May* that its spout hit her side, noisy as a volley of stones. The experience of being in the water with the whale was running in Michael's veins like a fever. Fear and exhilaration raced around inside him, tangled together, so he wasn't sure what he felt. So now, when it tried to tip him out of the boat again by putting its head under the stern, he clung on with both hands, his knuckles white and his heart beating hard in his ears. After a moment or two the whale stopped trying. Michael wondered if the clicks told it that he was afraid.

It swam slowly around the boat, very close, and Michael grew calmer and more curious, until the desire to be in the water with the whale overcame his fear. He tied the painter to his ankle, put on his snorkel and face mask, and slipped over the side.

Now it was the whale's turn to be alarmed. It jerked in the water like a startled fish, and jinked downwards. Michael floated on the surface, his face submerged, the rope snaking back to the boat, and looked down at the whale below him. It swam on its side, the sunlight just strong enough to dapple its skin. The speckled white around its narrow lower jaw made it look like it had been eating mouthfuls of flour. Michael could see its eye, clearly looking at him. It swam horizontally under the boat, perhaps twelve metres down, and then turned and swam back on its other side, looking at Michael with its other eye. He remained still, trying to keep his breathing through the snorkel as quiet and regular as possible.

Then the whale headed back towards the surface, bending its long body and pirouetting along its length. It curved as it rose, to arc under where Michael floated, so that it was swimming belly up, perhaps three metres below him. The movement was so graceful, the creature so flexible, so perfectly controlled and yet free, that Michael found himself thinking of hummingbirds and the way they cruised between flowers, changing direction with effortless precision. As the whale passed beneath him, he felt the wash from its tail, and saw the patchy detail of its skin, where more sections had stripped away, leaving the whale's belly looking like a badly painted wall.

Michael's vision was limited by his mask, so he couldn't see where the creature had gone. He took a breath at the surface, then paddled himself around, feeling awkward in the water compared to the whale. He looked back to where the *Louisa May* floated, connected to him by the umbilical cord of the mooring line. The whale was hanging in the water a few metres below the boat, tail down, head up, clicking. The boat looked so different seen from below – a little scoop of green hull, and the metal twist of the propeller poking downwards. And it struck Michael that the world above the water was as unknown and unknowable to the whale as the dark ocean depths were to a human being.

As he watched, the whale took the drooping rope in its mouth, and for a moment he thought it was going to bite through it; but the whale was just finding out what it was, like a baby putting something between its gums. It was so gentle that Michael hardly felt the tug. It let go of the rope and headed towards him. Michael took a deep breath and dived. He couldn't go down very far, but for a moment at least he wanted to break that connection with the surface; to meet the whale in its own world.

They swam towards each other, and at the last second the whale turned, that effortless pirou-ette again, so that it was almost within reach. It stopped still, and Michael did his best to do the same. The whale managed this without any appar-ent effort, but for Michael it took a lot of flailing arms and legs.

Belly up, both the whale's eyes could look at Michael at the same time. They squinted around its jaw like someone peeping round the side of a house. A loose piece of skin bigger than a sheet of paper was floating beside its head, but still just attached. With the last of his breath, Michael propelled himself further down, too close to the creature's underside for him to see its eyes. But the whale kept still, trusting his intent. He caught hold of the irritating bit of skin, so fine and slick; it slipped and came apart in his fingers, but he managed to pull most of it free. At once, the whale turned so that now one eye lay almost under Michael's hand, and looked at him for a long moment.

There were black spots in Michael's eyes. He'd never held his breath for so long or gone so deep. The surface was a long way away, and it took willpower to breathe out all the way up to protect his lungs from damage. He burst back into air and took a deep breath. How must a whale feel after an hour down there? He put his mask back under the water. The whale had dived: he could see the cylindrical body fading into the blue below him, a strange being from that other world.

Just think of the mysteries they see down there, Michael, at the very bottom of the sea!

Yes, just *think*. Was the whale thinking the same thing looking at the strange little creature from the unknown world above the surface?

He knew that a wild animal would never come when it was called, like a dog, but the whale was now so special to him that he *had* to name it – even if only in his head. It didn't take him long to find a name: Freedom.

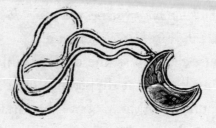

12

Michael got to the hospital late and found Gran's bed empty. The sheets had just been stripped off and lay in a laundry bag at the foot of the bed. He sat down on the mattress, feeling his knees give way and his head swim. There could be only one reason why Gran was not in her bed. On an evening he had been delayed, she had died.

A nurse he'd never seen before, small and skinny – the exact opposite of the familiar Sister Taylor – came up to him with a big smile.

'Didn't they tell you at reception?' she said, still beaming.

Michael wondered how anyone could be so heartless as to smile at such a time.

The nurse looked at him carefully. 'She's OK,' she said. 'She's been moved to a private room. I'll show you.'

Michael didn't ask any questions; he was still reeling from the shock of having believed, if only for a moment, that his gran was dead.

She was propped up on a whole mound of fluffy white pillows, in a room with a TV and a big window looking out over the town. She opened her eyes when he came in and raised the thumb of her right hand. That little bent thumb was so hopeful, so obviously trying to cheer him up, that it wrung his heart. Her forefinger roved around a little, pointing to the room. Michael understood at once.

Look at this, Michael, the finger was saying. *Looks like your old gran lucked out at last!*

'Michael!' she breathed. 'Michael!'

He was so glad that she had said his name, not Davis or Samuel or Ivor.

'So good to see you!' she said. Her voice wasn't much more than a whisper, but her eyes were bright and full of life.

'How are you doing, Gran?' he asked.

She smiled and opened her eyes wide in the old Gran way. 'Oh, I'm on the mend!' she said. 'Be out of here any day now.'

'You take it steady, Gran,' Michael chided her gently.

'I don't want Davis paying any more bills than he has to.'

Michael's heart dropped with disappointment. She was still confused after all.

But Gran nodded her head. 'Davis! Davis is paying for this room! He called the hospital today.'

Then she let go of Michael's hand and went limp as a rag, as if the effort had worn her out. In seconds she was fast asleep, snoring her usual purring snore.

It was almost time for work at the Flying Fish. Wearily, Michael got up and walked down the corridor.

'Michael! Michael?' It was Sister Taylor, just leaving at the end of her shift. 'Great news about your uncle, isn't it?'

'My uncle?'

'Didn't your grandmother tell you? Davis Fontaine called today and made a bank transfer to pay for all her treatment and a private room!' She saw the look on Michael's face. 'It must be a great weight off your shoulders,' she said kindly.

'Did he say where he was calling from?' Michael asked.

'No – no, he didn't. I'm sorry.'

'He left Liberty before I was born,' Michael explained. 'If he calls again, could you ask him to contact me at the restaurant where I work, the Flying Fish?'

'Yes, I know it. I'll tell him.' Sister Taylor put her hand on Michael's arm. 'Are you OK?' she asked.

Michael nodded and stumbled away, not sure what he felt most: relief that the bills would be paid, or disappointment that it was the uncle he had never met, not his father, who had suddenly appeared out of the blue.

The moment Michael stepped through the door of the Flying Fish, Eugenia burst into the kitchen with a huge tray of dirty plates.

'Oh, am I glad to see you!' she said. 'Malady's off sick and I've never seen the place so full!'

Michael took the tray. 'Just what I need,' he said. 'An evening of being too busy to think!'

'Don't tell me you ever *think*, Michael Fontaine' – Eugenia grinned – ''cos I know *that* can't be true.'

She waltzed out of the kitchen, and in spite of everything that was racing around his brain, Michael found he was smiling.

People were earning good money on NME's construction sites, and they all seemed to be in the Flying Fish that night to spend it. Michael and Eugenia didn't get a moment's peace: they cleared tables *and* took orders *and* washed up until almost midnight.

Finally things calmed down a bit, and as Michael was collecting dirty glasses from the bar, he overheard Mr Joseph's conversation with his two most regular customers, Rooseveldt Dringo and Miss Eliza Harmany.

'What I want to know,' Mr Joseph was saying, 'is who this JJ is. Could be some criminal, for all we know!'

'Oh, don't be so suspicious, Errol!' Miss Harmany scolded. 'Maybe JJ is a movie star who wants to keep his identity secret.'

'You taken a look at how fast that Marine Exhibition Centre is going up?' Mr Dringo whistled through his teeth.

'Marine Exhibition Centre for *what*? That's what *I* want to know,' Mr Joseph said as he poured their drinks. 'Why doesn't that Spargo or his boss – whoever *that* is – *tell* anybody?'

''Cos it makes a better splash in the news if it's a surprise.' Miss Harmany rolled her eyes as if it were obvious. 'Don't you know about marketing, Errol?'

Mr Joseph wasn't convinced. 'Maybe,' he said. 'And *maybe* he doesn't want anyone knowing what it's going to be until it's too late for anyone to object!'

'Oh, don't be such misery,' said Miss Harmany, waving her red-nailed fingers around and flicking her hair.

'Well,' said Mr Dringo, 'it *is* kinda weird. Doesn't look like a regular building at all. More like a big old . . .' He struggled for the right word, but Mr Joseph was ready with one of his own.

'*Tank!* Like a great big *tank!* And what would you keep in a tank that *big*?'

'I dunno.' Miss Harmany giggled nervously. 'A whale?'

Michael suddenly felt cold, and Spargo's gravelly voice growled in his memory: *All our plans depend on you. Find those whales.*

Mr Joseph pulled something from a drawer under the bar. 'Take a look at this,' he said. 'Friend of mine got it for me. His son works on the new fish market site. It's the packaging they're getting ready to use.' He slid the plastic wallet with its printed label across towards his friends.

'Well, I can't read a word of it!' Mr Dringo said, sipping his beer.

'Course you can't, Rooseveldt.' Miss Harmany laughed, and pushed the packet back across the counter. 'It's Japanese! Now, Errol, what's suspicious about that? Everyone knows they eat a lot of seafood over there!'

'I'll tell you what's suspicious,' said Mr Joseph, getting cross. 'They have two million of those packages. I mean, how many fish do they think are in the sea around Liberty?'

'Well, I'm glad,' she said, getting quite heated herself, 'because my two sisters have got jobs at the fish plant starting right after Carnival, and two million packages is work for a long time!'

'OK . . . What about this, then? They're keeping the packages in a *safe*. A *safe*, for fish packs? I mean, what do they want to keep so secret?'

Inside Michael's head things began to make a picture; he couldn't see yet what it showed, but he knew it made him feel uneasy. While Mr Joseph argued with Miss Harmany, he slipped the plastic package with its Japanese writing onto his tray with the dirty glasses.

Back in the kitchen, the chefs had gone home; Eugenia was getting ready to leave.

'Wait a second!' Michael called.

'Are you kidding?' she snapped back at him. 'If I stand here a moment longer, I'm going to fall over.' She was almost out of the door and showed no sign of staying.

Michael hesitated. *Don't rely on another soul, then you don't owe nobody a thing*, Gran's voice said inside his head, but he couldn't get to the bottom of his suspicions about Spargo alone. He swallowed his pride. 'Please, Eugenia,' he said quietly. 'I need your help.'

He saw her think of some clever put-down to fire off at him, but she didn't say it. Instead, she came back into the kitchen and perched on one of the stools. 'OK,' she said warily. 'What?'

He pulled the fish-plant packaging out of his

pocket and gave it to her. 'I need to find out what this writing says.'

Michael watched as she examined the package. He could almost hear her brain clicking away.

'It's Japanese,' she told him.

'Yeah,' he said, 'and your mum works for a Japanese guy now, so . . . Can you help?'

Eugenia frowned. 'If you tell me *why* you need to know, I'll help!' She smiled the sassiest of her sassy smiles.

'O-K . . .' Michael said slowly. 'I'll walk you home and tell you on the way. But I don't want to hear that I'm stupid for not working things out on my own.'

Eugenia nodded. She looked almost sorry, Michael thought, but he was probably mistaken.

Michael had been reluctant to admit his suspicions even to himself, but hearing the talk about the tank in the Exhibition Centre and the mysterious packages in the safe had made them impossible to ignore. All that, plus Spargo's odd desire for secrecy and his strange, threatening manner all added up in Michael's mind like a line of figures. Telling Eugenia about it lasted all the way down the Old Town road to the other side of Cat's Paw. They stopped under the one streetlight at the end of Eugenia's street.

'So you think there's something bad about that big tank they're building at the new Exhibition Centre?' Eugenia asked.

'I don't know,' Michael said, shaking his head, 'but it's like a whole lot of jigsaw pieces that are starting to make a picture. There's something about that guy . . . just makes me suspicious.'

Eugenia shrugged. 'But he's crazy anyway,' she said, 'because there just *aren't* any whales around the island any more.'

'That's what I thought,' Michael told her, 'but it's like Spargo *knows* that there are whales here somewhere. Like he has some kind of secret information.'

'Or he could just be an old fool . . . ?'

'Yeah,' Michael said, 'I told myself that too, but then . . . there's another thing you should know.'

He took a deep breath. 'I found a whale. A sperm whale.'

'Wow!' Eugenia exclaimed. 'So d'you think there are more?'

Michael nodded. 'Sperm whales are pretty sociable – that's how the old whalers used to catch so many.'

'So why was *your* whale on its own?'

Michael shrugged. 'I think his family could be around here. But he was kind of exploring. My dad said that's what young males do. He was so curious, like he wanted to find out about me. He tipped me out of the boat so I was in the water with him.'

'You *swam* with a *whale*?' Eugenia gasped. 'What was it like?'

He frowned and thought hard. 'It felt like . . . like the beginning of the world. Like I was the first person and he was the first whale, in the first ocean.'

Eugenia stared at him. 'Well,' she said at last, 'Michael Fontaine is a poet. Who would have guessed?'

Now it was Michael's turn to be speechless.

'Would you take me?' Eugenia asked. 'Take me to see your whale?'

'Well,' Michael spluttered, 'I don't know . . .'

'Mum gave me a camera for my birthday – just a cheap throwaway one,' she said, 'but it might help to get some pictures, to prove there really *are* whales before Spargo does anything bad?'

She was right. It might help.

'OK,' he said. 'Can you be at Golden Cove by eight thirty tomorrow?'

'I can,' she replied, 'and I won't even have to miss school. It's half term this week!'

Eugenia almost danced up the street when they said goodbye.

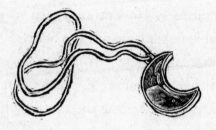

13

She was late. It was almost nine, and the builders were already hard at work by the time Eugenia arrived; they watched as she got into the *Louisa May*. Michael guessed that they had been told to make sure he stuck to all Spargo's conditions about the use of the boat. He didn't care. As soon as he had shown Eugenia the whale and got some pictures that would help prove what Spargo planned, he was going to quit anyway.

'I'm sorry I'm late,' Eugenia said. 'I had to call in at my cousin's to ask her to cover for me if we're late back.'

Michael cast off and turned the *Louisa May*'s

nose out to sea. He was surprised to see how comfortable Eugenia was in the boat.

'You aren't the only person who knows about boats, Michael Fontaine!' she said when she saw him watching her coiling the mooring lines and stowing them away. 'My grandpa used to take me fishing when I was little.'

Michael headed directly north, and then turned west to the deeper water a mile or more offshore, where Freedom had last dived. The water wasn't the glassy calm it had been for the last two weeks: the swells grew like great deepening breaths, and the wind picked up. Still, Eugenia seemed at home in the boat, and Michael was quietly impressed.

For two hours and more he motored up and down, stopping every so often to scan for signs of a spout. He grew more and more anxious, afraid that Freedom wouldn't appear.

'It was right around here that I last saw him!' he told Eugenia.

'It's OK, Michael,' she said. 'The whale's got

the whole sea to swim in; no reason he should be in one spot.'

But he could see that she was disappointed, maybe even wondering if he'd made the whole thing up. How could he prove to her that the whale *was* real, and how important Freedom was to him?

The medallion! Now that he was bringing her to meet Freedom, it felt like she was already part of the secret anyway. Michael stopped the engine and sat beside her.

'I want to show you something,' he said. 'It's a secret I've never told anyone.'

He pulled out the medallion and put it in her hand. 'My dad gave it to me. It's half of a riddle that the old whalers used to find whales. Kind of directions where to find them.'

Eugenia was fascinated; she looked keenly at the silver crescent, and read the words engraved beneath the whale's head.

'I thought Peter could be Morne Pierre,' Michael explained, 'and it would hide the Devil if you saw it from a certain position. Except I don't know what the Devil could be.'

Eugenia's face lit up. 'Don't you remember in history? Morne Liberty was renamed when the island got its independence. It used to be called Morne Diabolo! Devil Mountain!'

That was it! If only he'd paid attention in class he could have worked that out! Michael thought.

'You'd have to be beyond Cape Paradis for Morne Liberty – Diabolo – to be behind Morne Pierre,' he said excitedly.

'But that would only give you a direction, wouldn't it?' said Eugenia. 'Not a single position.'

She was too clever, that was for sure, but she was right. The two mountains would line up, one hiding the other along a line that could stretch for miles north of the island.

'Maybe the other half of the medallion tells you how far on that course you have to go . . .' Michael said thoughtfully.

'Maybe it says something else too . . .' Eugenia

pointed to one of the tiny words. 'Have you ever wondered why it says "*when* Peter hides the Devil", not *where*?'

Michael looked at her in astonishment. He'd never thought of that.

'Sperm whales wander around, don't they?' she went on. 'But maybe there's a time of year *when* whales gather, and maybe that's what Spargo knows . . .' She frowned. 'Who has the other half of the riddle?' she asked.

'My uncle Davis, who I've never met. My dad never knew what the other half said, because he and my uncle didn't get along so well.'

'But didn't you say he's paying your gran's hospital bills? So you could ask him what his part says.'

'Except he's been in England for years, and I have no idea how to contact him,' Michael said.

They sat in silence for a few moments.

'Could we try out the first bit of the riddle?' Eugenia asked. 'See if we can at least find the course you'd have to steer for Peter to hide the Devil.'

'Yeah! We could. Looks like my whale isn't here anyway.'

Without another word Michael turned the *Louisa May*'s nose to the north.

The swells grew, and the surface of the sea broke into choppy waves. But the *Louisa May* was a sturdy little boat, and Michael was sure he could keep her safe. Further and further north they went, but still Morne Diabolo peeped from behind Pierre so that they looked almost like the twin peaks of one mountain.

Michael looked ahead: the sea to the north was much rougher, and white caps were visible on the horizon.

'We're getting pretty close to the channel up here!' he told Eugenia.

They both knew what that meant. The channel lay between the island and her neighbour to the north. The water there was open to the wild Atlantic, with waves and winds that had two thousand miles of ocean in which to gather strength. Out in the channel was no place for a little craft like the *Louisa May*.

'We could try just a little further, though, couldn't we?' Eugenia said.

There was no doubting her nerve, Michael thought. 'OK,' he argued. 'Maybe another half a mile.'

It was slow progress. The wind grew much stronger as the *Louisa May* lumbered her way amongst the swells and growing waves, and it took all Michael's skill and concentration to keep her on course. Waves broke over her side, and Eugenia baled with the plastic carton Michael kept in the boat for that purpose. It was time to turn back. Michael steered round, and faced south again. It was too much of a risk to go further.

Ppppppfffffffff!

A dark, blocky head spurted a blow from its top corner, and a log-straight back wallowed in the waves: a sperm whale. Then another and another, their spouts making slightly different sounds as they popped through the dark blue surface.

PPPPFFFF!

Pppphhhhffff!
Pwwwafffffff!
PPPPFFFWAAA!

Eugenia cried out in delight and surprise, and immediately began clicking away with her little camera. The whales were so close that even its tiny lens would show them clearly.

In amongst the hills and valleys of the roughening sea, more whales were surfacing! Their black snouts exploded with the first loud breath after a deep dive. The *Louisa May* was surrounded by more than ten sperm whales. Michael and Eugenia stared around in wonder, hardly able to believe that they were in the middle of a whole *school* of whales.

'I think you're a whale charmer!' Michael told Eugenia. She laughed and took some more pictures.

Although it was hard to judge the size of the whales, some were definitely bigger than Freedom, and one was much smaller. They gathered together, twenty metres in front of the boat, a mass of lolling giants, water sluicing over and between them. Slab-like noses appeared, crinkly expanses of dark grey flank and pale speckled undersides, with long, U-shaped jaws showing under the surface. Pointed corners of tails, the flat paddles of flippers, a jumbled flotsam of dark shapes.

The whales rolled around each other, on their sides, on their backs, tail up, tail down, making use of every bit of the three dimensions that their watery world afforded them. They clicked so that the hull rang with the sounds.

Then two more whales surfaced on the edge of the group. One had a yellowish scar shaped like a target on its back, and its spout made a noise unlike the other whales', as if some musical instrument had got stuck inside the blowhole.

Weeeeepffffff!

The other whale swam very close beside it, and when they turned together, Michael saw Freedom's four white scars! This must be his family! This big flute-blowing whale could be his mother!

'That's my whale – Freedom!' he cried. 'He's the one I swam with!'

The children were as mesmerized, as enchanted as if they had been whisked away by the angels who had stolen poor So-So's wits. For what might have been hours, they watched the whales lolling and rolling around together. There was no more room left on the camera. Eugenia rolled it up in a thick plastic bag and put it in her backpack to keep it dry.

Then, as if a signal had been given, the chaotic milling about ended, and the log-like backs and huge heads lined up side by side, blows all going in the same direction, right into the wind. Almost as quickly as they had surfaced, they dived again, Freedom next to the big squeaking whale that Michael assumed was his mother. Their tails rose out of the water long enough for him to see that some, like Freedom's, were perfect triangles, while others were scratched, torn or misshapen. Big Squeaky's tail was so worn away that one side was like the prongs of a fork. It struck Michael that Freedom was being raised by an elderly lady, just as *he* was. One after another they slipped down under the surface with not even the tiniest splash, and were gone.

The children recovered their wits and looked around. They had followed the whales for quite a way, paying no attention to where they'd been headed. In front of them, far too close, were the white-capped waves of the channel, wild and frightening. When Michael turned back to see if he had at last reached a point where Peter hid the Devil, he saw that the island had disappeared behind a cloud like a huge purple bruise. A squall was racing towards them across the sea, and the little *Louisa May* was already floundering in the swell, a long, long way from a safe harbour.

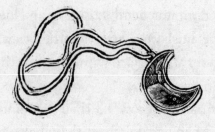

14

Michael had never been out in such rough seas. His father had always been cautious. If the sky looked wrong, or if there was any report of a storm, he'd stay close to land or haul their boat up the beach at Cat's Paw and not put out to sea at all. In his eagerness to show the whales to Eugenia, Michael had been careless, and now their lives were in danger.

Eugenia set to constant baling as Michael did his best to steer a course that would take them back towards the shore, where the wind and waves would lessen.

'How bad is this, Michael?' Eugenia asked, looking up at him.

'Bad!' he replied. 'But I'll get us through, I promise.' He never liked to make promises he couldn't keep, but he didn't want her to be scared.

In minutes, the waves had become angry fangs, their tops drooling foam like spittle. The *Louisa May* was more like a surfboard than a boat. Rain fell, curtain after curtain of it, blue-grey and hissing into the sea. The island disappeared, and the boundary between air and water rubbed to a blur. Water streamed over them, making their clothes stick to their skin, running into their eyes. The wind was racing in from the Atlantic, blowing hard from the north-east. It ripped into them, stealing their heat until their teeth chattered. Michael clamped his hand to the tiller and tried to hold a course.

The compass was in his pocket. He guessed Anse Gabrielle was east-south-east, so that was where he had to aim. The beach lay beneath Morne Pierre, the highest part of the island. This was the most sheltered stretch, the nearest calmer waters. But steering directly for Anse Gabrielle would put the boat parallel to the waves; to avoid this, he had to zigzag to and fro, trying to keep in the right general direction, but feeling that in spite of his efforts the wind was pushing him away from the island.

The waves grew higher, the wind stronger, the sky darker. Rain and waves. Eugenia kept baling without a word of complaint, but water was getting into the outboard too. It began to sputter and misfire. Without an engine to keep her moving forward, the *Louisa May* would be spun round by the wind and hit with the full force of the waves. They would sink in moments.

It was time to switch to the back-up engine.

'Eugenia, I need you to steer while I start the other engine.'

For the first time she seemed unsure, but he showed her how to hold the tiller, and she gripped it tight with both hands.

Michael pulled on the cord of the second engine with as much sudden energy as he could. Every nerve focused on the lovely sound of the engine starting up, but the sound did not come. He pulled again, almost bursting with the effort. But the result was the same. Nothing. *Nothing*. It was dead, completely dead. And then the first engine finally died.

Until the moment when both engines failed, Michael had kept his nerve. Kept the fear at bay. Just done the next thing that needed doing. But now he looked round at Eugenia's frightened face; at the sea and sky closing in like a trap.

Sometimes in a storm you can't even think of getting back to shore. Sometimes you just gotta survive till it's over and you can see where you are. Somewhere from deep in his heart, his father's voice spoke. *You just gotta survive till it's over.*

Oars. He didn't have an engine, but he did have oars and he was a strong rower; had been even when he was little. His father had always said so.

Michael leaped into the middle of the boat. 'We got to row,' he shouted. 'Quick!'

They had to fit the oars into the rowlocks fast; with no engine and no oars, the *Louisa May* would be turned side on to the waves and the next big breaker could simply flip her over. Michael struggled to release each oar from its mounting under the gunwales. He could see the next big wave coming for them, gathering itself, ready to pounce. The *Louisa May* tipped and rolled, and Eugenia sat there, frozen with fear. Michael knew that, alone, he wouldn't have time to fit both oars before the breaker reached them. He dropped one on the bottom of the boat and wrestled the other into the rowlock. It seemed to be fighting with him as much as with the sea and wind, but just as the big wave struck, he got it into position. He held onto it, bracing it like a rudder, pushing the *Louisa May*'s nose into the wave so she had some chance of slicing through it and not being engulfed. Aware of the huge power opposing him, he closed his eyes, fighting it with all his strength. The little boat faltered, tipped, quivered, and then . . . the wave was past, and in the small moment of calm he fitted the other oar into the rowlock and began to row.

Eugenia came to her senses; shakily, she moved to the middle of the boat and picked up the other oar, fitting it into the rowlock. 'I can take one,' she said quietly. 'We'll do better that way.'

They pulled in silence for a few minutes, finding their rhythm, then Eugenia said, 'You just saved our lives and I was no help at all. I'll never tease you again.'

Michael smiled. 'I couldn't stand that!' he told her.

They rowed on, the rain running down their faces and the spray making their eyes sting; then Eugenia shoved him with her shoulder. 'Good thing you can row,' she sighed, "cos you're so stupid!'

There was no thought of steering a course. All they could do was try to keep the boat's nose into the waves, so as not to capsize. They might make it to the shelter of the island if they could just keep afloat for long enough.

They had rowed for what had seemed like hours,

while the sky and sea had a tantrum around them. Sometime after dark the storm had passed and the clouds cleared. The shape of the mountains stood out against the starry sky, and Michael could see that they had been blown south, but not as far out from shore as he'd feared. He pointed the *Louisa May* towards Morne Matin and rowed, while Eugenia curled up, exhausted, in the bottom of the boat, clutching her bag with the camera and its precious film.

Michael grew too tired for thinking and rowed almost in his sleep. But some instinct, like the force that brings turtles across thousands of miles of ocean to the little beach where they hatched, worked inside him and brought them back to Cat's Paw.

The water close to shore was calm and littered with the flotsam that the storm had stolen and blown into the water: leaves and branches, broken bits of boat and fishing gear. Through this, the *Louisa May*'s hull shushed onto the sand. Someone gently pulled the oars from Michael's hands and laid them in the boat. Dimly, Michael came to his senses as So-So helped him out.

'I *feel* you coming over the sea to me,' he said. 'Only So-So awake at this hour watchin' over people's dreams – not even Pascal on the beach this long before dawn.'

So-So helped Michael and then Eugenia up the beach. He sat them down by his little fire, wrapped them each in a blanket and handed them chipped mugs of hot, sweet tea.

Michael wrapped his hands around the mug. The sugary tea tasted wonderful, and he felt the tangle of waves and wind clearing from his mind. He glanced at Eugenia, and she smiled over her mug and breathed, 'Glad we're still alive!'

'Told you we'd make it!' Michael said softly.

'But you didn't believe it when you said it.'

Really, Michael thought ruefully, Eugenia was way, way too clever.

So-So topped up their tea, and fed them beans, heated in the can on the fire. The children wolfed them down; nothing had ever tasted quite so good in all their lives.

'It's getting light,' Eugenia said. 'I must go to my cousin's house. She won't cover for me if she wakes up and finds I didn't get in last night.'

She got up, thanked So-So and gave him back his blanket. She looked completely recovered, just a bit damp still. Michael was amazed; he felt his legs wouldn't quite support him if he tried to stand up.

Eugenia leaned down to say goodbye. 'I'll see if I can get the film developed today,' she whispered. 'We'll talk at the Flying Fish tonight.'

Then she was gone, running down the coast road under the streetlights.

Michael ate two more cans of beans and several mugs of extra-sweet tea, and began to feel better.

'You are not quite restored, my brother star,' So-So said, looking at him keenly. With a single deft slash of his machete, he opened a coconut and handed it over. 'Drink now. Drink. Then sleep!'

But Michael's mind was too wide awake for that. 'I'm far on the other side of sleeping now, So-So.'

'Then, Samuel's boy,' he said, 'we will talk. Quiet quiet so you mind is not troubled.' He put some more sticks on the fire, along with two more cans of beans.

'Now,' he began, his expression both stern and kind. 'Here are some things I know: that I promise Samuel I will keep you safe. And here you are, all but drownded in a storm. That you would not steal a boat, and yet this boat you couldn't pay for. What I wonder,' So-So went on, his head on one side, 'is what does the person who give you this boat want in return?'

As always, he somehow knew the truth at the heart of things. Michael considered telling him all about Spargo, but So-So would worry too much, so he said, 'Too much – so today, as soon as I've been to see my gran, I am taking this boat back. Then, So-So, you won't need to worry.'

So-So put the end of one finger on Michael's

forehead and said sternly, 'I can see see just how much worry I *do* need, and I see you cannot take back this boat without engines. So I will fix the outboards.'

Michael clasped So-So's hand as he'd seen his father do many times. 'Thanks, my friend,' he said. 'Thanks!'

He walked down the coast road as the light spilled over the top of the island. He would go and see his gran; then he would go to Golden Cove and drop off the boat and leave a note in the tin on the fridge, saying that he no longer wanted to work for Spargo and his pretty boss.

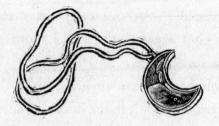

15

It was hours too early for visiting time. Michael took the lift to the third floor, and went straight to Gran's room before anyone had a chance to tell him off.

She was wide awake, sitting up and looking out of her window. He could see at once that her mind was as clear as the new day.

'Michael!' She beamed at him and then immediately frowned. 'Why aren't you getting ready for school? Your clothes are a disgrace, boy!'

For a second Michael's mouth opened like a landed jackfish; then he remembered what Eugenia had said about the holiday. 'It's half term,

Gran,' he said. 'No school today. I'm going fishing with Mr Loubière at Cat's Paw. Get some fish so I can grow some more!'

'Oh Michael!' Gran smiled at him. 'You grow any more you won't fit in the house. Come now, sit here.' She patted the bed, and obediently Michael perched beside her.

'I love this room, this view,' she said. 'Look at how beautiful it is!'

The window framed the treetops of the Botanical Gardens, which glowed in every gorgeous shade of green in the bright early sunshine. Below them, the little houses stretched around the blue of the bay, and beyond that you could see the curve of the wooded headland to the south. Gran was right: it was beautiful. Michael looked into her face, lit up with delight, and thought how little time there had been in Gran's life to sit and enjoy the beauty around her.

'I'm so grateful to Davis for paying for this,' she said. 'He was a wild, wild boy, but it proves he came good in the end. I wish he'd come here.

And Samuel . . . I want to see my sons.' Gran never cried, but now her eyes were shining with tears.

Michael wished her sons, especially her younger son, would come too. But he didn't know what to say except, 'I'm here, Gran.'

'You are. You are,' she said. 'And Sister Taylor told me you paid my first hospital bill. I *dread* to think how you did *that*. Not swimming with sharks, I hope, Michael?' She glanced sideways at him, her eyes sharp and enquiring.

Michael had to look away. For the first time he felt truly ashamed of the bargain he had made with Spargo. All along he'd known something was wrong.

A trolley was clattering along the corridor, bringing the patients their breakfast. 'You better go, Michael,' Gran said. 'That Nurse Martinez who brings our breakfast is a terror. She scares me!'

Nothing and no one had ever scared Gran, but now she seemed so tiny and frail.

'Bye, Gran,' Michael said. 'Take care!'

'No, *you* take care. I worry about you.' And she looked right into him – so far it hurt.

Michael smiled his best smile and hurried out. He didn't want her to see him cry.

Outside the hospital he looked out at Rose Town. The streets were strewn with leaves and flowers that the storm had thrown about. It gave the place a sweet, rather innocent feel, as if the roads and houses had just arrived in the middle of a garden.

But down at the Marine Exhibition Centre the cranes clanked and the jackhammers shouted, as Spargo's construction, with its giant metal tank, took over the whole of the waterfront. It was certainly big enough to hold a whale.

Suddenly, just returning the boat and walking away with a few pictures of Freedom and his family wasn't enough. Michael decided he must find out for certain what Spargo planned so that people could stop it before it happened.

He would tell the old man that he had found the whales; even take him to find Freedom. This would be the bait to draw him out so that he would show who, and what, he really was.

It was still early enough to catch Spargo at the Rathborne. Michael slipped past the doorman and left a note at reception saying he had *swum with a good friend and met some family. Meet at Golden Cove?*

Then he bought batteries from the shop next door to the bakery on Marlin Road, and ran all the way back to Gran's house. Under her bed, in a paper-covered box, he found what he was looking for: the small cassette tape player Samuel had bought her years ago that she had never used. He inserted the batteries, said, 'Testing, testing,' into its little microphone a few times, and played it back. It was a shock to hear his voice; it didn't sound a bit like he expected, but it proved that the thing worked. He shoved it in his sweatshirt pocket and went back to Cat's Paw.

So-So had worked his magic and was patting the engines, which were now back on the boat. 'Easy fix!' he said with a smile.

Samuel had always said that So-So was the finest mechanic in Liberty, if only people knew it.

They didn't speak any more as they launched the little boat. But just before Michael was about to start the outboard, So-So looked keenly into his face. 'I am here, star brother. Always here. Remember.'

For all So-So's strangeness, Michael was grateful for this; he smiled at So-So and clasped his hand quickly before puttering quietly away. As he left Cat's Paw behind, he remembered he'd left the bait box with the compass and the log book by So-So's fire. It didn't matter – he wouldn't need them today. He headed straight out until he was far enough from watching eyes to be just another boat shape against the bright surface, then turned north, towards Golden Cove.

Michael had never seen any other boats

moored in the cove, but now there were four big, powerful motor boats moored side by side at the jetty, all black, with tinted windows. They looked like weapons. The sight of them made him want to leave his boat and run, but it was already too late for that. Spargo was waiting on the jetty; he pulled the *Louisa May* close with a boat hook and secured her mooring line. Then he ordered Michael out.

'I take it you've found us a whu-ale?' Spargo said when Michael was standing next to him.

Michael nodded. 'Up north, almost in the channel.'

'You were out there yesterday in that storm?' Spargo exclaimed.

'For part of it,' Michael said coolly. He wanted to appear as calm and capable as possible, when really his heart was racing and the cassette recorder sat heavy in his pocket. A figure stepped out of the shadow of the boathouse and came towards them.

Michael recognized her as the woman who'd

got out of Spargo's car at the Rathborne: JJ in person.

'JJ, meet Michael Fontaine,' said Spargo.

The woman was older than he'd thought – about Mrs Thomson's age – and was dressed in jeans and sneakers. She was pretty, but her face was stony, as if it didn't know how to smile. It reminded Michael of the Siamese cat that a neighbour had once owned. He'd often watched the creature solemnly chewing up small birds with the same expression that JJ now wore. But just as Spargo concealed his cold nature with forced jollity, so JJ too smiled at him now.

'It's nice to meet you!' she said. She spoke quietly, and her hand, when he shook it, was small and soft. Once again Michael had the feeling that somehow he knew this woman. It was very disconcerting.

'So,' JJ went on, 'are you going to take us to meet your whales?'

'I can try!' said Michael, giving her his best fish-selling smile. 'I'd like to hear more about NME's plans for the whale watching too!' He tried to sound casual, but he noticed JJ looking at him carefully, as if someone had told her about bait having hooks inside as well. He began to think that his plan to entice them to talk about their real plans and to secretly record them was ridiculous, but it was too late to turn back now.

'Right, then,' said Spargo. 'Let's get going, shall we?'

Spargo and JJ climbed aboard the *Louisa May* with all their gear – waterproofs, cameras, food, and a walkie-talkie too. Bigger boats had radios to summon help from shore if they got caught in bad weather or if an engine failed. But most island fishermen couldn't afford such a luxury. If you got into trouble, you got yourself out of it or you drowned, like Michael's grandfather had.

'I have every confidence in your abilities as a skipper, Michael,' Spargo explained. 'But with a lady on board we must be able to summon assistance if we need it, eh?'

As they cast off, he tested the radios and held

a brief conversation with someone on one of the big motor boats.

'On standby, sir,' the voice on the radio crackled.

'Await instructions. Out,' Spargo replied.

Michael wondered what that meant. It sounded ominous. Another of Gran's sayings surfaced in his mind: *Swim with sharks and you get bitten.*

Well, he was swimming with two sharks now, that was for sure.

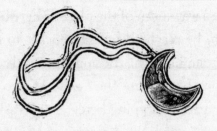

16

With all the extra weight, the *Louisa May* made slow progress. JJ and Spargo sat quietly on either side of the bow, obviously used to boats. JJ was definitely the boss. It was strange to see big, square Spargo bending his head to listen respectfully to her.

Michael played the part of boatman and 'whale guide' as best he could. He steered extra carefully, as the sea further from shore was still rocking and rolling a little after the storm. He pointed out landmarks, birds, a turtle, a distant school of dolphins, talking loudly over the noise of the engine to get their attention. Neither Spargo nor JJ took much notice.

Quite a way south of the places where he'd seen Freedom, he reached into his pocket to turn on the recorder, knowing the engine would cover the click. Then he brought the *Louisa May* to a stop.

'Why are we stopping here?' Spargo asked.

Water slapped the bottom of the boat, but otherwise there was a silence that made Michael nervous.

'I'd like to hear more of your plans before we go any further.'

'Are you trying to bargain with us?' JJ asked.

'No. I just want to know a bit more before we get to where I usually find the whale,' Michael blustered.

'Usually?' snapped Spargo. 'So you've found whales more than once, have you! You've been keeping that from me, lad. Not what we agreed at all!'

'Nor was taking that girl in the boat yesterday,' said JJ.

Once again she looked like a cat who'd caught a bird. She moved to sit beside Michael in the stern. Of course, he'd forgotten: the construction workers had seen Eugenia.

'It was just fishing,' he told them. 'I never told her about the whale.'

Spargo now moved from the bow so that he too was sitting close to Michael on the other side of the tiller. It was as if the pair of them had planned to do this.

'You see, Michael,' Spargo said, 'I don't think you have been quite honest with us. I'm not *sure* if you've seen a whale or not, and if you have, who you've told. But I *am* sure you have some information we need. I've been waiting for you to *give* me that information. But now we're going to have to *take* it.'

JJ reached into her bag and pulled out a curved sliver of silver on a chain. She held it up for Michael to see the sperm whale's tail, and the tiny writing. He knew at once that it was the other half of his medallion.

'Such an honest boy!' JJ said. 'I can see from your face that you know exactly what this is. Your uncle – or should I say, my brother-in-law – gave this to me. Well, I took it, anyway, when he was dead.'

Michael stared at her.

'Yes, that's right, Michael,' she told him. 'Your long-lost mother. You don't seem very happy to see me.'

That's why she had seemed familiar. Deep down inside, his baby self remembered her, his mother – the mother who had left him almost as soon as he was born.

And now she said that Davis was dead. So who had rung the hospital? Who had sent those cards at Christmas? Michael's heart felt as if it had swollen to fill his chest. Breathing was difficult.

'Where is the other half of this medallion?' JJ's voice was still quiet, but razor-sharp.

All along . . . all along, when he had thought he was laying a trap for these two, he'd been walking into the one they had laid for him.

'My dad's got it,' he managed to say.

'No' – JJ shook her head – 'he hasn't.'

164

Michael hated the way she said that, so final and so knowing. A flare of anger rose inside him. 'What have you done with my father?' He leaned towards her.

The boat lurched, and JJ cried out. But it wasn't Michael's doing.

Shhhhhrrrrrrchhhhhhh.

Freedom's flipper scraped along the underside of the boat as the whale lifted the little craft very slightly, then dropped her again.

Pwwwwffffff!

His spout blasted the starboard bow of the *Louisa May* with the stale fishy smell of his breath. His big square head poked out of the water and he began to swim around the boat, investigating the two unfamiliar passengers with rapid clicks. First he swam one way and then the other, showing the dark eye and the four white scars on the right side of his head.

JJ and Spargo were transfixed in a way that gave Michael the shivers and made him think once more of cats and their prey.

'Our lucky day!' JJ breathed. 'Looks like he was telling the truth after all.'

Spargo looked at the young whale with narrowed, careful eyes. 'About six years old, I'd say. Not independent yet, so his family won't be far away. And he's very comfortable around this boat.'

He gave Michael a grim slit of a smile. 'Well done, lad. You've made a very good job of befriending this animal. He should be very easy to catch.'

JJ pulled two walkie-talkies out of a bag and handed one to Spargo. 'Call the chopper,' she said, 'and the catcher boats.'

Spargo nodded.

'If we work fast, we could have it in the tank by midnight.'

Michael shook his head in horror. He had led Spargo and JJ straight to his new friend, who was now swimming around the boat, as curious and friendly as ever. Michael reached for the outboard starter cord: a sudden engine noise might frighten

Freedom away in time. But of course Spargo and JJ were sharks, well used to slicing up little fish like him. Michael didn't even see Spargo's fist; he just found himself on the bottom of the boat with blood running into his eyes.

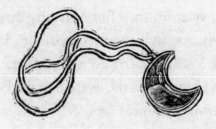

17

The four boats that had been moored at Golden Cove sped towards them, as streamlined and menacing as barracuda. They spread out in a line like well-rehearsed dancers, and stretched a huge weighted net between them – a wall blocking the whale's retreat to open sea.

The young sperm whale had picked up the roar of their engines minutes before they appeared. He had dived, but resurfaced after just a few minutes, only metres away from the *Louisa May*. Michael guessed that Freedom found the little boat reassuring, like the presence of another whale.

Michael was lying in the prow of the boat, his

hands and feet tied; the blow he'd received sent bolts of pain through his head. With JJ's help, Spargo had tied him up and taped his mouth. He now lay with his feet and hands lashed to the boat and his head jammed into the prow. Spargo had covered him with a sack.

'Don't want my crew getting jumpy about the kid,' he said. 'They don't see him, they won't ask questions.'

Michael's left eye could just see a sliver of daylight between the sack and the top of the gunwale, so he could watch the ghastly ballet of boats unfold.

Spargo steered the *Louisa May* slowly after the whale – not too close, not too far, just enough for the familiar shape of the boat to make the whale feel that all might yet be well.

'He's young,' Michael heard Spargo telling JJ. 'All he knows about boats is what he's learned through being close to this one. He doesn't understand what danger he's in.'

Michael screamed through his gag when he heard them both laughing at this.

Very gently, Spargo coordinating their movements with the walkie-talkie, the boats pushed Freedom closer and closer to land, away from the deep water where he was comfortable. They never got near enough to really spook him, but his clicks would tell him all about the large net preventing his escape. Little by little it drew in: first an arc, then a crescent, and finally a closing C, with the whale and the *Louisa May* at its centre.

All this took a long time, but the last and most horrible part happened quite quickly. Spargo steered the *Louisa May* out through the small gap in the C, and the speedboats closed it behind her, rapidly tightening the ring of the net. Over the revving of their engines and the sound of an approaching helicopter, Michael heard Spargo yelling instructions.

'Pull the bottom of the purse tight now!' he told the men in charge of the net. 'Get the divers in!'

Freedom's blows were closer together now as his breathing grew shallower with stress. He dived, but must have found the net closed and moving up, forcing him towards the surface. It was like a vice cinched around the whale, holding him tight so that he could no longer turn round or up-end, only thrash his tail uselessly.

Six men in wetsuits and diving gear went over the side of one of the boats and swarmed around the whale, marking the net with flags on buoys for the helicopter crew to home in on from the air.

The sun had sunk towards the horizon; the sea was turning from royal blue and turquoise to navy. Blood blossomed in the water around the whale and tinted the vapour of his spout a pale rose colour, as he was chafed and cut by the nets, and battered his tail against the boats. In the low, slanting light, his head was black and shiny as polished jet, the white scratches standing out like chalk marks. He looked suddenly vulnerable, surrounded by the aggressive boats, the chopper hovering, hawk-like, and the shoal of purposeful divers.

'Lower the sling,' Spargo ordered over the radio. 'Steady now. Keep between the buoys.'

Something like a vast grey bandage dangled from the dark mouth at the side of the chopper and was lowered into the water. The divers guided it around the whale's middle. This took several attempts, and more blood blossomed as Freedom thrashed around in desperation.

But at last the huge sling was around his body and the helicopter winched up the slack cables until they were taut. Now it could begin to take the whale's weight, but it hesitated. Michael saw the crews, the divers and Spargo all look from the whale up to where the chopper hovered, as if suddenly realizing what a huge task it faced. He squeezed his eyes shut and wished that the cables would snap, the net would tear, or that the people now so intent on doing this terrible thing would just stop, stop, *stop*, and let his friend go.

But it was only a small pause in the nightmare . . .

Spargo was shouting to the pilot and crew of

the helicopter in the walkie-talkie: 'We've done the calculations. We know it'll take the weight. Do it! *Just do it!*'

Slowly the helicopter rose and took the strain, until the sling had lifted the whale out of the water, the dark mass of the head showing at one end, the great triangular tail at the other.

The sun dipped below the horizon, and the last peach-coloured light spilled over the sky. Below the helicopter swung the whale, out of his home, his element, his tail beating uselessly. Michael could only imagine his terror. Nothing would make sense. Nothing would be familiar. It would be like madness. It tortured him to even think about it.

'Take it straight to the tank,' JJ ordered over the radio. 'Spargo will alert the Rose Town crew.'

The chopper wheeled round and headed south, with two of the black boats speeding along beneath it. The shape of the captured whale shrank into the growing dark and the sound of the rotor blades faded.

Michael slumped in the bottom of the boat, his head pounding. He was beginning to drift out of consciousness . . . Then he heard the other two speedboats drawing up to the *Louisa May*, one on either side. There were voices – a mixture of Spanish and English: Spargo and JJ giving orders in two languages. Someone walked across the *Louisa May* and stepped off onto the other boat, which then cast off; the sound of its engine retreated, and faded to nothing. Now there was just the quiet slap of water and the low bumping of two boats rafted side by side, the *Louisa May* and one other. Michael was alone with Spargo and JJ once more.

Spargo pulled off the sacking and untied him from the boat, so although his hands and feet were still bound he could sit upright. Spargo propped him in the bow and threw a bucket of seawater over him. Michael opened his eyes and saw the pair of them sitting amidships looking at him. Light from the black boat moored alongside slanted over the *Louisa May*.

'Good work, Michael,' Spargo said. 'We'd never have got that whale so easily if it weren't for you. But like I say, now we need more information . . .'

'The medallion,' JJ said, and ripped the tape from Michael's mouth.

He shut his eyes again.

'Look, Michael,' she went on. 'NME, Spargo and I – we've done a lot for Liberty. People are grateful. Nobody will care if one little old lady dies in hospital or some smart-arse schoolgirl goes missing. So tell us where the medallion is.'

After everything he'd witnessed, Michael was sure JJ meant what she said. He felt faint; he knew he couldn't stay conscious for much longer, but he lifted his bound hands and touched his chest.

JJ gasped. 'It's *on* you? He had it on all the time – you could have just taken it, Spargo, you idiot!'

She leaned forward and pulled the string from under Michael's neck band; he felt the medallion slide off his skin. She held it up to the light.

Michael watched her lips mouth the familiar

words. 'That's it!' she exclaimed. 'Davis gave us the time, and now we know the place!'

'We can have the packing plant up and running as we planned,' Spargo said. 'We'll have those first two million packets ready in no time!'

'And the visitors will be flooding to see the captive whale at the Exhibition Centre,' JJ added. 'So many jobs in Rose Town will depend on us that no one will dare get in our way! My profits will be huge.'

'*Our* profits,' Spargo corrected her.

'Of course. Yes.' JJ smiled at him. 'I should never have doubted you, Spargo.'

It was like being a mouse listening to cats discuss how they'd bite your head off. Michael's eyes closed and the words drifted over him, almost as if they were no longer anything to do with him.

'What shall we do about the boy?' Spargo asked.

'He's been every bit as useful as we hoped.' JJ could have been talking about the battery life on the walkie-talkies. 'But now that we have this information, I don't want to risk anyone else getting hold of it or knowing where it came from.'

'You *sure* about this, JJ?' Spargo's voice rasped. 'I mean . . . he's your own flesh and blood, your son: murder is not something we should take lightly.'

JJ's reply was as sharp as shattered glass. 'I've seen you take murder lightly enough in the past, Spargo,' she snapped. 'I never was mother material, as my mother-in-law was so fond of telling me. This is business. That's all.'

Spargo sighed. 'As you like. Pass me the gaff there, would you?'

The *Louisa May* was a tough little boat and her planks didn't want to spring apart and let in water. But Spargo was strong and the metal of the gaff irresistible. With no more than ten sharp blows she was holed, just below the waterline.

'There,' he said, recovering his breath after the effort. 'That's a decent little hole. Won't sink her for a while – plenty of time for us to get away.'

JJ retied Michael to the inside of the boat. 'One more thing before we leave,' she said. 'Now that I know what they both tell us, it's best if these go to the bottom with . . . the boy.' Her voice caught a little on the last two words. She put the strings of both halves of the medallion around Michael's neck.

The *Louisa May* lurched twice as the two of them climbed up into the speedboat. Then there was a roar of engines, and at last, quiet. The only sound was the trickle of water slowly filling the bottom of the boat.

Thoughts slopped about in Michael's head, disconnected and confused, as he slid in and out of consciousness. None of them made any sense. The whale suspended in the air. JJ *his mother?* Water – water in the bottom of his boat? The *Louisa May* would fill and sink, and he was tied to her, so he would drown. It didn't seem to matter that much.

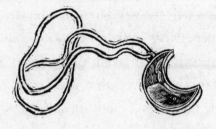

18

There was a whisper underneath the boat. Something large moving there. A gentle touch. A probing stream of clicks.

Michael's face was partially submerged, the water washing around the side of his head and cooling the place where Spargo's fist had struck. The water had been covering his mouth a while ago, almost up to his nostrils on one side, but now he was breathing through his nose, and through the little hole he'd managed to bite in the tape over his mouth. He sputtered. The water level was falling; he could feel it creeping away from his body. Perhaps, he thought vaguely, he wouldn't drown after all.

He opened his eyes. The moon was low in the sky and the stars swam up and down on the dark water. He realized that the *Louisa May* was no longer floating: something solid was holding her up – Freedom? For a wonderful moment he thought he had been dreaming, and that his whale was still free, and now visiting him as before. Then he remembered. But if it wasn't Freedom under the boat, gently lifting her, then who was it?

Pffff! A whale blew close by.

Sspffff! – another.

Ppppffsss! Another.

Weeeeepffffff! A fourth, quite different from the rest; a squeaky blow, as if the whale had a flute caught in her blowhole . . .

There were splashes around the boat, signs of giant bodies moving smoothly in the water. Michael remembered the day of the storm, and the whales that had approached the boat – Freedom's family. They'd come looking for him and found the *Louisa May* instead. He tried to look around the boat, but he was bound too tightly, and his head filled with blackness once more.

When his eyes opened again, the moon was gone. The boat was still being supported, and he heard blows and gentle swooshings of water around him. He felt a little stronger and, by biting and pushing with his tongue, freed most of his mouth from the tape. Faint and far away in the dark, there was the sound of an engine, a single puttering outboard. It came closer and closer.

The whales heard it too. Michael could feel their anxiety in their puffing blows and the streams of clicks, as if they were discussing what to do.

With a shushing scrape, the *Louisa May* was lowered back onto the water. There were four more deep outbreaths, and the surface sighed as the great flukes lifted and sank. The whales slipped down, and were gone. Immediately water began to trickle back into the boat, more quickly than before.

'Michael!' Voices called across the water, faint and distant but clear.

'*Michael!*' It was So-So and Mr Joseph!

But another voice was calling too: 'Michael! *Michael!*' *Eugenia?* Eugenia Thomson!

Sheer astonishment pulled Michael free of the last cobwebs of unconsciousness; coughing and spluttering, at first he called out almost too weakly to be heard.

'Here!' It didn't sound like much of a word, smothered by the flapping edge of the tape on his mouth. He tried again, more loudly this time, feeling the strength return to his voice: 'Here! Hurry!'

Their approach was agonizingly slow. They were too far away to hear his voice over the outboard, so they had to stop, listen, then come closer, stop and listen again. The water in the boat was several centimetres deep already. It wouldn't have to fill the *Louisa May* to make her sink. Even half full, her gunwale would be under the surface, and then she'd go down in seconds.

'Sinking!' he yelled.

'Swim, Michael!' Eugenia yelled back.

'Can't. Hurry!'

Everything had come back with Michael's consciousness. The terrible throbbing pain in his head and the places where the rope was biting into his wrists and legs; the agony of knowing what had happened to Freedom; and a fierce, fierce determination not to die. The call and response, call and response between his friends' boat and himself built and built, faster and faster, as the water flooding into the *Louisa May* approached its deadly tipping point. There was a terrifying crescendo when the only thing Michael could do to increase his chances of staying alive was to keep up a constant loud screaming, a wordless animal sound, made of fear and pain.

Then there was a blur of action and terrible anxiety as the boat reached him; blinding light from a torch; engine noise; the buffeting of a boat; Eugenia shouting, 'He's tied in!'

In the torchlight, Michael saw his friends'

expressions switch from hope to terror as they realized that, even now, right next to the *Louisa May*, they might still lose him if he couldn't be cut free.

So-So held the two boats together, and Eugenia and Mr Joseph slashed frantically at the ropes tying him, their hands groping blindly under the water. But Michael realized it wasn't fast enough: he was still firmly tied to the *Louisa May*, and any second now . . .

The sickening *scllooop* came as the boat's gunwale went under. The water rushed in. So-So's arms, as strong as steel, held onto Michael, but they were now also supporting the whole weight of the *Louisa May* and the water inside her. Mr Joseph and Eugenia carried on trying to cut him free. Michael had never heard Mr Joseph curse, but he cursed now, and Eugenia cried. Still So-So held him, silent, straining, his breath coming in more and more laboured gasps as the water-filled *Louisa May* pulled, pulled, *pulled* at So-So's boat, trying to bring her down too, as if the goal of all water was to drag the whole of creation down into the depths.

Through a blur of fear and horror, Michael experienced a moment of absolute calm: he saw that he must not take his friends down into the darkness too. With the very last of his strength, he wriggled and pushed them away to free them from the sinking boat. It made Mr Joseph and Eugenia lose their grip on him and propelled So-So backwards. But So-So had not let go, and the sudden backward wrench broke the last strands of rope holding Michael to the *Louisa May*. As the rescue boat rocked back onto an even keel, Michael was scooped into it, on top of his friends.

For a moment all four of them lay in a breathless tangle; then Eugenia said, 'This is positively the last time I *ever* get in a boat with you, Michael Fontaine!'

Michael told them who had tied him to the boat, and about the whale – caught and lifted from its home to go into the tank in Rose Town. They might not have believed him, had they not heard the helicopter flying by in the dark and seen a huge shape dangling below it. He didn't repeat what he'd learned about JJ – that she was his mother. It seemed too strange and too horrible. He even wondered if the blow to his head had sent him a little mad and he'd imagined it.

They wrapped him in a blanket and propped him up and told him to stop talking and rest. The boat belonged to Mr Dringo; like her owner, she was solid and old and rather wide. She chugged along, comforting and safe, with Mr Joseph and So-So taking turns at the tiller, and Eugenia in the middle with Michael. Even the darkness around the boat seemed friendly, and the way her faint stern light picked out the outline of his friends' faces. Eugenia held a bottle so that he could drink some water and fed him bits of cold fried fish from the restaurant. It seemed to him that he had never drunk or eaten anything so good. He crunched through the cold crispy crust into the sweet flesh, and felt so glad to be alive. He closed his eyes and listened while Eugenia explained how they had come to his rescue.

'A nurse at the hospital – she's a customer of Miss Harmany,' Mr Joseph said. 'She told Miss Harmany that your gran was worried about you. That you hadn't been in to see her this evening.'

'And I know you've been to see her very nearly every night,' Eugenia chipped in.

When Michael hadn't come to work, having agreed to meet Eugenia at the Flying Fish – 'to talk about the photos and the fish package and all' – she had begun to worry more. 'I was so worried, I had to tell Mr Joseph everything.'

'Then So-So came looking for you and said he had a bad feeling about you,' Mr Joseph added. 'So we shut the Flying Fish and borrowed Rooseveldt's boat to come look for you. So-So got its engine to start for the first time in two years!'

'I had your little black book,' said So-So, 'so I could see where you been mostly. So that is where we look.'

It was like a relay race, with each person taking up the next bit of the story. As they spoke, Michael realized that, all along, people had been looking out for him: not only the friends he knew about – Eugenia and Mr Joseph and So-So – but all the people he didn't know – from the nurses at the hospital, who knew quite well that he wasn't as old as he'd claimed but didn't want to get him into trouble, to the bus driver friend of Mr Dringo who had noted his journeys to and from Golden Cove. Nothing in Rose Town was ever really invisible: eyes had been watching and hands held out, ready to catch him.

They were quiet for a while, lost in the drone of the engine, then Eugenia said, 'What I don't get is why they wanted to *kill* you?'

She was right, Michael thought. What *was* so important about him that they wanted him dead? JJ's icy voice came back to him: *Best if these go to the bottom with the boy.*

He opened his eyes and sat up. He reached into the pocket of his shirt and pulled out not one but two medallions: his own familiar crescent moon, and another, smaller oval.

'I'm not sure,' he said, 'but these are something to do with it. Where's the torch?'

Eugenia shone it on the medallions in Michael's hand. In the white torch light, he showed how the two pieces fitted together to make one whole moon.

'This one's mine,' he explained to Mr Joseph and So-So, showing them the crescent shape. 'Dad gave it to me before he left. He said the other half was Davis's—'

Michael stopped in the middle of his sentence. Had JJ said that Davis was dead? Or was this some other dream created by the bump on his head?

'You OK?' Eugenia asked.

He nodded and went on, 'JJ knew about my half. When she found I had it, she and Spargo acted like it was treasure or something. Then she put them round my neck so they'd go down with me.'

So-So and Mr Joseph looked at each other and

shook their heads. Eugenia squinted at the tiny words. '*When Peter hides the Devil and . . . the angels kiss the lions' bite,*' she read.

'Surely guidance for a boat,' said So-So, 'from the days of the old whalers. Peter is Morne Pierre.'

'And the Devil is the old name for Morne Liberty,' said Mr Joseph.

Michael wondered whether he was the only person on the island who hadn't known this fact.

'Dad said that it was the way to find a place where there were lots of whales . . .'

Mr Joseph slapped his hand on his leg. 'Well,' he said, 'at least now we know what they were up to with all that building. It's *all* about whales, just like the bad old days. A whale *show* and a plant for packing whale *meat*. Two ways to make dirty money!'

Michael sat up as if he'd been given an electric shock. It was what he'd feared, but to hear it said aloud was awful. 'Whale *meat*?'

'Of course – you don't know!' exclaimed Mr Joseph. 'Tell him, Eugenia.'

'That package you gave me,' she said, 'with the Japanese writing? The guy Mum works for at the university – he translated it all, but the big letters just say *Whale Meat*.'

'*That's* why Spargo and JJ want to find whales,' Mr Joseph told him. 'To fill two million of those packs!'

Michael rubbed his throbbing head. 'Oh, I don't know,' he sighed. 'Maybe this riddle stuff is all crazy. Maybe it's just a story . . .'

'Spargo and JJ don't think so – that's pretty obvious,' said Mr Joseph. 'Your ancestors went out on the old whaling ships, Mikey. Maybe what the medallions say is true?'

'And the old whaler men *knew* things,' So-So added, tapping his head with one long finger. 'They killed thousands of whales, but Mother Nature, she recover if you give her a little space.'

'So I've just helped them to find whales and kill them,' Michael said miserably.

'They tried to murder you, Michael,' Mr Joseph told him kindly. 'And now we have the same information they do. So if there are whales to be found, we can find them and protect them.' He slapped his hand on the boat's side for emphasis.

'We just need to work out what the words mean,' said Eugenia.

Michael looked at her face, which was lit by the halo of dawn showing over the island. He could see her thinking; he thought he might hear her too if only the engine weren't making so much noise.

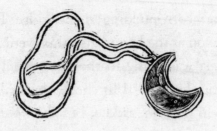

19

If Spargo and JJ found that Michael wasn't at the bottom of the ocean with the *Louisa May*, they would, as So-So said, 'want to finish the job for sure'. So the fewer people who knew where Michael was now, the better. Instead of going home to his gran's house, he went to Eugenia's. To cover her second all-night boat trip, Eugenia had told her mum that she was staying at her cousin's again to finish their Carnival costumes, so she didn't come with him.

She suggested he hide in the shed until her mum had left for work with Mostyn, then let himself in by the back door: 'Key's under the mat, and there's corn pudding in the fridge. Rest up. I'll meet you at the Flying Fish this evening.'

Eugenia was going to the library. There was something she needed to check, she said, and it might help with the riddle. But she wouldn't say what.

Michael was anxious to see his gran, but it was impossible for now. Mr Joseph had gone to the hospital to explain that Michael had a little touch of flu and wouldn't be in to see her today. If any of the nurses asked about him, he would tell them that Michael was 'missing' but not to worry Gran with it yet. That way, if the grapevine *did* reach JJ and Spargo, they wouldn't be suspicious. And So-So was going to 'see how the land lie, what is the word on the street', whatever *that* meant. Michael had a funny feeling that it might prove to be very useful.

They had all agreed that it was too danger-ous for Michael to go to the police. New Marine Enterprises were building a new police station and providing new uniforms. Nobody was going to listen to some kid telling a crazy story about an attempted murder by the two most important people on the whole island. The newspaper was sewn up too: *Sponsored by New Marine Enterprises* had appeared across the top of every front page since Spargo donated a new printing press. All Michael could do was sit and wait, and hope that his head would stop throbbing, and that he – or someone – would think of a plan to stop JJ and Spargo, and set Freedom free again.

He sat at the kitchen table eating corn pudding, with the photos Eugenia had taken with her little camera in front of him. They weren't going to win competitions but you could see that the whales were real. Not that the photos helped any more. Spargo and JJ were now several moves ahead in the game.

The house was very quiet, but it was noisy inside his head. He turned on the radio to balance things out a little, and heard Spargo talking! His voice was rich as honey cake as he played the jolly Cornish fisherman. If Michael hadn't been so hungry, he would have choked.

It was obvious that JJ and Spargo hadn't wasted a moment making up a good story to cover the sudden appearance of the world's first captive sperm whale in the Rose Town Marine Exhibition Centre.

'*The young whale is an orphan,*' Spargo's buttery voice explained to the presenter. '*One of our boats just came across him at sea. Without his family he'd die, so it was an act of mercy to bring him into captivity.*'

'*How can you be sure he's an orphan?*' the presenter asked.

Spargo gave a chuckle like Santa sharing a joke with his elves. '*I'm an old hand with whales, me boy,*' he laughed. '*Been studying them for more years than you been alive. So I know a lone youngster when I sees one. And now he's safe in our care, people from all over the world can come and see him!*'

'*Does this mean that there are whales in island waters again after so long?*'

'*Oh yes, I'd say so,*' Spargo replied. '*I'd say there's plenty of whales out there. More'n enough for the island*

196

to be making the most of them again. Why shouldn't you make money out of your ocean?'

'Are you suggesting a return to whaling?'

'Why not? We can harvest these whales sustainably and make Liberty the richest island in the Caribbean!'

'Well, that's a lot to think about . . . Thanks for coming in, Mr Spargo . . .'

'Ah now, lad . . . none of that "Mister" – just plain Spargo, remember?' Michael could hear the matey wink even without seeing it.

'Thanks, Spargo! I'm sure the visitors will be flocking to see the young whale at the MEC.'

'We'll be open from ten this morning, and all through Carnival. Look forward to seeing you all. Soon the whole world'll be coming to Rose Town to see our sperm whale!'

Michael pushed his bowl away. The thought of Freedom held in a tank had finally killed his appetite. He was too agitated and his head still hurt too much for him to rest, even though he couldn't remember when he had last slept. Just waiting around was impossible. He could at least go and visit his friend in prison. After all, Spargo and JJ were unlikely to be on the door, and they expected him to be fish food this morning. However, one of their thugs might recognize his shirt and shorts, so he would have to change his clothes.

There was a laundry basket full of clean clothes on the kitchen counter. Gingerly Michael began to look through what was there. Mostyn's shorts and T-shirts were tiny, Mrs Thomson's flowery dresses a bit like tents. Michael had hoped that some of Eugenia's dad's clothes might be around, but he didn't visit very often. The only things that would fit were a pink T-shirt that he had seen Eugenia wearing, and her navy-blue school skirt.

Michael sat back. He couldn't go out in girl's clothes. Supposing someone saw him? And then he told himself that this was the whole point. He wouldn't *be* Michael Fontaine wearing girl's clothes, but a *girl* – a girl who nobody could put a name to – and that was a good thing. He laughed to himself: if Spargo and JJ expected to see him at all, it was as a *dead boy* washed up on a beach. Not a *live girl* right on their doorstep!

He found a straw hat with a ribbon and a brim that covered his face. His flip-flops were fine; everyone wore those. The T-shirt felt just like any T-shirt, as long as he didn't think about the colour . . . But the skirt felt, well, just *wrong*, and on him it was pretty short. In some parts of the world men did wear skirts, he told himself – sarongs and kilts. All the same, he had to walk ten times around the kitchen before he had the courage to step outside the door, and even then he only managed it by thinking *very* hard about Freedom, trapped inside a tank.

Michael hurried through town, his head down. The shops were putting up decorations in their windows in preparation for Carnival; the streets were full of islanders who had come home for the biggest event of the year. A taxi driver he didn't recognize called out, 'Hey, darlin'!' to him as he turned down a side street towards the MEC. Michael clenched his fists and walked even faster.

There was a long queue outside the Exhibition Centre. Mothers with children too small for school, old folks and tourists. One old lady tutted at Michael and said something about how no daughter of *hers* would have been allowed out in a skirt *that* short. He pulled his hat down even further.

The entrance was very modern, all glass and chrome. Michael knew the two women taking money for tickets on the door: he had met them in Miss Harmany's. He whispered his request for 'one child ticket', and didn't look up, but inside the building the lighting was very low, and everyone was too excited about seeing the whale to look at anything else.

The 'tank' was shaped like a giant oil drum, set on its end, with wide glass panels going from the top, which was in the open air, down to the bottom, under cover. A big staircase snaked in a low spiral up the outside of the tank so visitors could look into the water at various levels.

Michael peered in through the first glass panel.

There were small lights in the bottom of the tank – just enough to show him that Freedom wasn't there. Cries of excitement up ahead, close to the top of the spiral staircase, showed where he might be. Michael squirmed his way up between the crowding people and came out into a big amphitheatre of seats at the top of the tank, overlooking the surface.

Pfff, pfff, pfff, pfff!

There was the familiar shiny dark head, with its line of scars.

But that was all that was familiar.

Instead of slow majestic spouts, these were short, nervous breaths. Freedom was bobbing up and down in the water amongst the dead squid that floated around him like so much trash tipped into a dirty pond. The tank was huge, but still little more than three times the length of the whale's own body. And as he was young and would grow every day, so every day that space would shrink.

Never before had the whale known any boundary except the ocean bed and the ocean surface. His movements had been limitless. In the sea, he had owned all the space around him, from shore to horizon and back again. Every breath had been taken at his own pace, as if he knew he was part of everything around him. That, Michael recognized now, was the source of the peace he radiated when they had met in the sea.

In less than twenty-four hours, Freedom had withered and shrunk, not in size but in spirit. He had become a *thing*, not a being; something dead rather than the most incredibly *alive* creature Michael had ever met.

Michael had half expected Freedom to be bashing his great head against the side of the tank, damaging both himself and his prison. He had heard stories from the old days of big male sperm whales smashing whaling boats to pieces. But this silent misery was worse. Even if he could have got close enough to call or touch the whale, what possible comfort could he offer that would make this nightmare bearable?

In despair Michael looked around. The faces were smiling or laughing. Why couldn't people see that this was wrong, horrible? Only one reflected his own horror and sadness. On the other side of the circle of seats, close to the exit, a man stood staring down at the whale; he seemed almost on the point of tears. Then he turned away sharply, replacing his sunglasses, and disappeared into the deep shadow of the doorway. Michael wanted to call out, but the man clearly didn't want to be noticed any more than *he* did.

Michael's heart jumped around in his chest.

Even under the beard and sunglasses he had recognized his father.

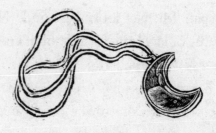

20

Everything about Rose Town was getting brighter and louder as Carnival approached. Michael walked through the bustle and noise of the streets in a daze. He had seen his father for the first time in almost seven years. He wondered if Samuel would even recognize him now. Certainly not in a skirt and a pink T-shirt! If he hadn't felt like crying, he might have laughed.

He leaned against the shady wall of the supermarket on Mile Street and thought. There were two places where he might find Samuel again: one was Cat's Paw, visiting So-So. But So-So wouldn't be there today; he was going to 'see how the land lie, what is the word on the street'. Mr Loubière or any of the guys on the beach would tell Samuel that. The other place was Gran's house. Was it really so dangerous to go there? Spargo and JJ thought Michael was dead, so they'd have no reason to be looking for him. All the neighbours had jobs, so there would be no one about at this time of day, and anyway, all sorts of strangers could be found wandering around the island at Carnival time. He decided to risk it.

He pushed himself away from the wall and began to run; then he remembered: it was Michael Fontaine who ran everywhere, not the gangling girl in the pink T-shirt; he slowed to what he hoped was a demure, though fast, walk.

He took a long route through the back streets, as the Old Town road felt too exposed. Then through the Botanical Gardens, up Garth Hill and out of town, cutting back through the banana plantation behind Gran's house, moving stealthily between the trees; or as stealthily as a boy can in a borrowed skirt!

He was just about to climb over the rickety fence beyond Gran's grapefruit trees when he heard voices and froze, crouching behind a thorny tangle of bougainvillea.

'Anything?' It was JJ.

Michael shuddered at the sound of her voice, and peeked fearfully between the leaves and flowers. She was perched on the edge of the bench on the veranda, not in jeans this time, but an elegant white suit and large film-star sunglasses.

That's your mother, he told himself, but he didn't feel that there was any truth in the words.

Spargo emerged through the door, unfolding his chunky body from the tiny, cramped interior. 'Not a thing,' he said, and sat beside her, pulling a pair of disposable gloves off his big hands. 'Nothing at all that could connect you with the lad. No pictures of you. Nothing written down. So your identity is safe.'

JJ sighed and adjusted her sunglasses on her pretty nose. 'Good. Very good,' she said in her usual business-like manner. 'I'll make sure the birth certificate goes missing from the Registry Office. And my people in London will take care of his father – as soon as they can track him down. The old woman will be dead soon anyway.'

Spargo looked out over Gran's garden. 'Nice little spot here!'

'Hmm. I didn't like it much as a young woman,' JJ said, 'but I'm warming to the place as a business opportunity.'

'Well, in five more days your opportunities will be opening up!' said Spargo. 'We'll have enough whale meat for the first shipment. And there'll be many more to come – and many more whales and dolphins to put into the Exhibition Centre. I'm starting to build three more tanks next week.'

'And in time we can expand the business,' JJ said. 'All sorts of things could be smuggled in and out of Rose Town with the whole population depending on us for their jobs.'

She got up. 'Let's go. I need to make sure our Carnival float will help keep everyone friendly.'

'And I'll need to be on board the *Ahab* shortly.

We must be in position by tomorrow night, according to the medallions! But first,' Spargo said, 'I think you need a spot of lunch, madam. Come along.'

Michael heard their footsteps going down the steps to the road, car doors slamming, the growl of an expensive engine, and then silence. He let out the breath he'd been holding and tried to take in everything he'd heard. What was all that about people 'taking care' of Samuel? Did JJ plan to kill his dad? It all chased around in his head like a pack of barking dogs. What should he do now? It was hard to think . . . Get some of his own clothes – *that's* what he'd do. He wasn't going to wear this wretched skirt and T-shirt for a moment longer.

There was nothing but the distant scribble of sound from town and birds peeping in the treetops; no cars approaching, no footsteps. Cautiously he climbed the fence and approached the door.

Spargo had turned Gran's neat little house where 'everything has its place', as Gran always said, upside down. Every cupboard had been emptied and every drawer overturned. Gran's old feather mattress had been slashed down the middle like a possum ready for the spit, and her small store of clothes thrown onto the floor. It was almost the last straw, and for a moment Michael wanted to wrap his hands around his head and wail like So-So. And then he remembered Freedom and his desperate shallow breaths – *Pff-pfff-pfff*; and his father's face disappearing again at the MEC.

No, *no!* He would *not* give in. He would *not* be afraid. He would get to the bottom of all this. Gran would be well. His father would be found. Freedom would be freed, and his family would *not* end up in little plastic packets.

Michael threw Eugenia's hat down on the floor and began putting things back into cupboards, slamming drawers and doors shut, stamping around the rooms. In fact, he made so much noise that he didn't hear footsteps on the path, or the screen door opening and closing.

'*Michael?*'

Of course, he knew the voice instantly, even after all this time. And, just as instantly, realized he was still wearing the skirt and pink T-shirt.

'They're Eugenia's,' he said, even before turning round. 'I had to have a disguise so Spargo and JJ . . .' He trailed off; when he saw his father's face, he doubted if Samuel had even noticed what he was wearing.

His legs felt like rubber, and he sat down without having planned to. His father came and sat beside him, and for a while they just looked at each other. Dad's bright, open face had clouded. There were wrinkles, lots of them, and streaks of white in his hair and beard.

Michael knew that his dad must also be counting up the changes in the son he hadn't seen in so long. When at last they spoke, they did it at the same time, and it took a few attempts to stop overlapping.

'You know who JJ is?' Samuel managed to get out.

That confirmed it. It *was* true. A wave of light-headedness washed over Michael. He couldn't speak, and had to nod his reply.

His father let out a long sad breath. 'It's not safe here, son,' he said. 'I've got a car parked on the other side of Garth Hill. Let's go.'

Dad was different. Harder. Quicker. And his voice had almost lost its island accent. He sounded English now. Like JJ. Like Spargo.

'Can't we clean up here?' Michael asked.

Samuel shook his head. 'No. They may come back . . .'

So he already knew about Spargo and JJ? There were a hundred questions on the tip of Michael's tongue, but his dad hustled him out of the door.

'Grab what you need, son, then we can talk somewhere safer.' Samuel's face was closed and anxious, almost the face of a stranger. 'I didn't want you mixed up in all this, but it looks like you already are.'

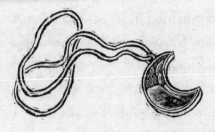

21

The car was a jeep with tinted windows like those on Spargo's car. Dad had never had enough money for a car when he lived on the island, but now he drove the jeep up the mountain roads and tracks as if he'd been born behind a wheel. He frowned at the road and didn't speak.

They drove up tracks that got rougher and more rocky and finally ran out in a clearing. A tiny cottage stood with its back to the forest; beside it a stream from the deep volcanic heart of Morne Matin bubbled and steamed over the rocks.

Samuel got two cold sodas from the fridge,

then they sat together on the veranda, sipping their drinks in silence.

'I owe you some explanations,' Samuel said at last, 'but it's hard to know where to start.'

Gran's voice popped into Michael's head; he looked sideways at his unfamiliar-familiar father, and said, 'Remember what Gran always says when you've got something to tell? *Come on, spit it out.*'

His father smiled, and it was a bit more like the old smile; the smile that made him 'Dad' again. He nodded and took a deep breath.

'Josephine left right after you were born,' he began. 'We'd been together for less than a year. Everyone knew what her family did in England: big-time drug dealers mostly. I hoped she was different, but she wasn't. She went back to the business; only ever came here to be out of the way of the police for a while.' He shook his head.

'I was young and foolish, and she was very pretty. What can I say?' Samuel sighed and went on, 'Anyway, a few years later, your uncle Davis got in touch out of the blue. First we'd heard from him in years, although I'd always made sure Ma got a card from him at Christmas – she never noticed they were posted in Northport.' He grinned suddenly. 'He wasn't a *taxi* driver, but he *was* working as a driver – for Josephine. She'd taken over the whole business, killed quite a few of her own relatives, it seems, and managed to make the whole thing look legal, so nobody could catch her.'

JJ was making a lot of money, Samuel told Michael, but she made enemies too, so he wasn't surprised when he heard that Davis had been shot.

'I never told Gran. Couldn't bear her to know that her son had come to such a bad end. That's why I went to England. To find out what had really happened . . .'

But when Samuel arrived, he found the British police waiting for him. They told him that JJ had had Davis killed; they wanted his help in exposing JJ's criminal empire. So he agreed to train as an undercover policeman and pretend to work for JJ!

'She didn't want to be my wife,' he explained, 'but she *did* seem to trust me enough to employ

214

me. I know now that she was just after the other half of the medallion all along.'

His father an undercover policeman? Michael could hardly take it in.

Samuel smiled at the look on his son's face. 'Bit of change from being an island fisherman,' he quipped with a fleeting spark of his old warmth, 'but the pay was better! I never expected to do it for more than a year or two.'

He went on with the story, and Michael tried to get over his astonishment and remember to close his mouth!

The more Samuel found out about JJ, the more he wanted to stop her. 'I became involved in the whole set-up. I just couldn't come home to you and Gran.' His face looked closed and sad again. 'I was afraid I'd be putting you in danger, even if I replied to your letter. Pretty soon JJ got together with Spargo. He's an old-fashioned villain. Would have been a pirate if he'd lived two hundred years ago. He'd disappear from London for months, then pop up again. All that time I think they were planning this operation in Rose Town.'

Michael could just see Spargo with a cutlass tucked in his belt, making people walk the plank.

'Spargo owns an illegal whaling ship, the *Ahab*,' Samuel went on. 'He kills whales and sells the meat – outside the law and very, very successfully. And just like JJ, he pretends to be a businessman, doing nothing wrong.'

Then JJ had started asking Samuel about his grandpa's past as a whaler; about the old riddle for finding whales.

'She'd got Davis's medallion. I guessed that much. That's why she had him killed. But I played dumb. I'd never showed her my half when we were married; she wasn't even sure I had it. Never trusted her enough for that. I told her that the whole thing was just a story,' Samuel said, 'and I believed that's all it was, but it made me wonder what she and Spargo might be up to, combining their two businesses. And when they *both* disappeared and I heard about New Marine Enterprises in Rose Town, I knew I had to come back and find out what it was.'

Michael's father had followed JJ and Spargo to the island, travelling under a false passport given to him by the British police.

'Daniel Paul' – he smiled – 'that's who I'm supposed to be. An IT engineer from South London, here for Carnival.'

Samuel had received Michael's letter, but he had to keep a low profile, so all he could do was contact the hospital pretending to be Davis and pay Gran's bills.

'I rang the hospital when I got to Rose Town,' he said. 'They told me you were missing. I had to find out what had happened, and when I got to Ma's and saw JJ and Spargo . . . I was very glad when I caught sight of you.' Samuel took a deep breath. 'And now I think you might have more pieces of this jigsaw than I have!'

Michael's brain was whirling. He wanted to lay out the story of the last few weeks carefully – like a map that shows how the rivers go round the mountains to the sea; how roads divide and lead to towns – but it swirled around in his head and wouldn't come into any sort of order. It all just tumbled out. Poor Mr Levi and the little blue boat. Taking the job to pay Gran's bills. Having to trust Spargo and his promises. Finding Freedom, and the terrible night when he was taken and Michael finally found out the truth about his employers.

It was hard when he got to the part about Freedom being captured because it made him feel so bad; and the part about being almost drowned because of the look on his father's face.

'Josephine is a monster,' Samuel said. 'I'm so sorry you had to find out like that! I'm so sorry I wasn't there to help.'

Michael saw that he and his father were the same: what hurt them most was not being able to protect someone they loved.

As Samuel listened, Michael saw the new dad, harder and sharper than the one he remembered. The new dad was very interested in details, like the whale-meat packaging and the fact that Spargo's workers were mostly Spanish speakers. He asked what JJ and Spargo had said; nothing seemed to surprise him.

Then Michael came to the hardest part of all, about the moon medallion and how he had given away its secret. Suddenly the old dad shone out like a familiar kitchen lamp showing through the cracks in a shutter.

'Don't feel bad,' he said. 'There's nothing to be sorry for, son.'

He took the two silver shapes from Michael's hand and fitted them together. 'Wow, I haven't seen these two together since I was a little kid. I couldn't read when Grandpa gave them to us. Davis never showed me his half of the medallion. For years I wasn't even sure he'd kept it.'

Samuel squinted at the words that ran across the moon's two parts. 'I must be getting old!' he said. 'Here, Michael, you read them!'

'*When Peter hides the Devil and the angels kiss the lions' bite,*' Michael recited.

His father shook his head and looked thoughtful. 'Hard to believe it means anything. Spargo and JJ must know something we don't. JJ's family were once harpooners. Maybe she's got some other information from her family.'

'Eugenia thinks she can work it out,' Michael told him. 'I was going to meet her at the Flying Fish with So-So and Mr Joseph. Could we go?'

Samuel's face hardened again, back into New Dad, and he answered solemnly, 'Well, they're already involved, just like you are, so yes, I think we should. Let's see if we can put this puzzle together!'

His eyes flashed the way they used to out in the boat, when they'd hit a big shoal of jacks. Then Michael knew that New Dad wasn't really so different from the old one. All along this new dad had been inside the old one, just as the more grown-up Michael had been inside the little kid in the boat.

They got back in the jeep and drove down the mountain towards Rose Town.

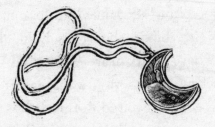

22

They arrived at the Flying Fish before Eugenia, but Mr Joseph and So-So were already there. So-So was overjoyed to see his old friend again, and Mr Joseph almost shook Samuel's hand off the end of his arm.

Samuel asked for the blinds to be drawn, and they all sat around the table speaking quietly, as if they could be overheard.

'I'm working for the British police,' Samuel began. 'We've been following the activities of Spargo and JJ – Josephine Jaquard, my ex-wife – for some time.'

Mr Joseph and So-So gasped together.

'JJ is Josephine!' exclaimed Mr Joseph.

'That girl.' So-So shook his head. 'I always know she have a dark heart. I always say—'

Samuel cut him short. 'I would rather none of you had become involved in this, but as you are, none of us is safe until Spargo and JJ are behind bars.'

Mr Joseph was bursting with questions, but New Dad Samuel's serious face made him hold them in. Instead he sat up very straight and said, 'The moment I saw Mikey tied into that sinking boat, I was ready to do whatever it takes to get the people who did that to him.'

So-So took in the information about Samuel's new profession as if he'd always known his friend would do something like that. He looked very serious, a warrior in a sequinned vest and running shorts. 'We will fight with you, my friend,' he said, 'no matter how strong the enemy. That Josephine always had a soul of wire and wickedness – bad, bad, bad.'

'OK,' said Samuel. 'So let's put together what

we know. Spargo wants a supply of whale meat, and JJ wants a base where she can make everyone depend on her for work and money. Somewhere small enough that she can control the law . . . so it won't matter what the law says about whales, for example. With so many people coming and going, and lots of exports, she can move the money from her crimes around easily.'

'So the island *could* be perfect,' Mr Joseph chipped in, 'if they can only find whales to hunt . . .'

'And if,' Samuel added, 'they can get the whole thing up and running so fast that by the time anyone thinks of opposing them, everybody's job depends on them.'

'Devils!' exclaimed So-So. 'And the more folks come flocking to see the whale in the MEC, the easier it is for their bad-badness to come and go!'

'Yeah,' Samuel agreed. 'It all fits . . .'

Bang! The back door of the kitchen slammed open. Before Michael realized what was happening, his father had leaped up and was standing beside the swing doors into the restaurant with a gun in his hand! With the other hand he pointed to the bar, motioning Mr Joseph, So-So and Michael to get behind it. They crouched by the glasses and bottles of beer. Seconds passed like days.

The swing door creaked, there was a little scream, and the sound of something heavy falling to the floor. It wasn't Spargo or one of his 'helpers', but Eugenia! Mr Joseph, So-So and Michael popped up from behind the bar like jack-in-the-boxes to see her standing amidst a pile of dropped books, shakily greeting Samuel, whose gun had now disappeared.

'Is it really you, Mr Fontaine?' she breathed.

Samuel smiled. 'Yes it is, Eugenia, but I'd appreciate it if you kept that very quiet!'

She looked at them all in turn. 'I'm sorry if I scared you,' she said. 'I had to kick the door open 'cos my arms were full of books!'

Michael helped her pick up the ones she'd dropped, and quickly explained about his father. Just like Mr Joseph, she was immediately bursting with questions, but she had news of her own.

'I've found out about the riddle!' she whispered. Michael could see her brain whirring and sparking behind her eyes. She couldn't wait to tell them!

The moment everyone sat down and the back door was locked, Eugenia began.

'The riddle isn't just about *where* to find the whales, it's about *when*!'

She pulled some papers from a blue folder and spread them out on the table with the books. 'The Peter hiding the Devil part is just the kind of navigation island fishermen have always used. Lining up the mountains and headlands to find their way around.'

'Yes, yes,' So-So said eagerly. 'You steer towards Morne Matin to get home to Rose Town!'

'Peter is Morne Pierre, just like you thought, Michael, and we know that the Devil is the old name for Morne Liberty.'

Eugenia showed them the name Morne Diabolo on an old map in one of the dustiest books.

Michael leaned over it to work out where the

riddle meant. 'To get Diabolo – Liberty – hidden behind Pierre,' he said, tracing it with his finger, 'you'd have to be right up here, almost due north of the island. Out in the channel!'

Samuel and So-So nodded in agreement.

'But what about the lion and angel part?' asked Mr Joseph. 'What kind of place is a lion's bite?'

'Sailors weren't good at spelling!' Eugenia said with the smuggest of smug smiles. 'The bite is really B-Y-T-E . . .'

'Right, 'said Mr Joseph eagerly. 'Like Josie's Byte off the east coast, between Port Maron and Mariette Island!'

So-So jumped up from the table and did a little dance. 'I know this place!' he cried. 'The Lions' Byte. Here, here . . .' he said, putting a trembling finger on a stretch of sea north of the island, where tiny dots that might have been spots of mould spotted the page. 'An old, old guy in Northport, he tell me one time of a fishing spot among rocks and tiny, tiny islands, called the Lions. Here between them is the byte!'

Eugenia waited for the little wave of excitement around the table to die down.

'But here's the other part of the directions,' she said, and laid another page on top of the map – a photocopy of dark handwritten words, with a passage underlined in red. 'It's a journal written by a man who came to the island on a whaling ship three hundred years ago.'

She read out what the underlined words said: '*The sailors have much lore and superstition, and notice stars and planets pertaining to their work and life. A harpooner on the ship* The Marqui, *one Silas Jaquard . . .*'

'Silas Jaquard?' exclaimed Mr Joseph. 'Could have been Josephine's great-great-great-grandpa!'

So-So nodded excitedly. 'C'mon, girl. Let's hear the rest of it . . .'

Eugenia went on reading. '*Um . . . one Silas Jaquard, told me of the three stars they call the Angels, which are much talked of, although they are but a faint spark in the sky, showing above the island's horizon for a few days each year. When these stars are*

227

positioned correctly in the night sky is a portent of a great gathering of whales, which come to feed each year on creatures swarming from the deep.'

'Angel on the lions' bite,' Michael said, 'must mean when the star shines on that stretch of water.'

Eugenia raised an eyebrow as if to say, *So, more brain than I thought, Michael Fontaine.*

'Yeah, but that's only useful if we know what the star is . . .' Samuel said.

'The librarian is pretty keen on stars and astronomy,' she explained. 'She knew about the Angels. They show above the sea for three days starting tomorrow night, the first night of Carnival. If we lined up the stars, Morne Pierre and the Lions, we'd be in the right place.'

Michael's eyes lit up. 'So we're ahead of JJ and Spargo!' he said eagerly. 'They can't have worked this out yet?'

Eugenia shook her head. 'Sorry. There's something I should have told you. The original journal had been stolen from the library. I think we can guess who was behind that.'

'That explains why they wanted your half of the riddle,' said Mr Joseph. 'They already knew the *when* part; they just needed the *where*.'

Michael sagged in his chair. He had given Spargo the last clue he needed to be able to find and slaughter Freedom's family!

'We have to stop them, Dad! We have to get Freedom released,' he cried. 'Can't you arrest them?'

Samuel shook his head, his face creased with worry. 'The island police are already in Spargo's pocket. Without their help there isn't much I can do until I get back-up from London and Interpol. That'll take a few days,' he told him.

'But what about this evidence?' said Michael, pointing to the whale-meat pack that Eugenia had brought with her. 'What about what they did to me?'

His father shook his head again. 'You can be sure the safe that pack came from will be empty, and JJ and Spargo will be on a plane to South America if they get even a hint that we're onto them. We have to lie low for a couple of days and catch them with whale meat in packs, and even then, if the police and the government in Liberty don't back us up, they could still get away with it.'

Samuel's face was grim and determined – the new undercover policeman dad; not the old dad whose face had brightened at the sight of dolphins and who'd invited Michael to think of the mysteries that whales might see at the bottom of the ocean.

'But Freedom's family will be *killed* if we wait!' Michael stood up, fists clenched. His father didn't seem to care that the whales would die.

'I can't risk Spargo and JJ getting away,' Samuel said grimly. 'I have to wait for back-up and catch them red-handed, or six years of undercover work goes for nothing.'

Father and son stood glaring at each other.

So-So put a hand on each of their shoulders. 'Wait, wait, my star brothers,' he said quietly. 'These monsters have big friends – police, radio, newspaper, airport people so they can fly away. But there is one thing they don't have: friends on the street, on the bay, on the water . . . ' He gave a sly smile. 'The ordinary poor man and woman, nobody bribe *us*, build *us* no road or headquarter, buy *us* no smart new uniform! Nobody bother to think of *us*. But we are very many, and we are everywhere, my brother and sister star. Nothing can happen unless we use the strength of our arm, the light of our eye. You know?'

Samuel looked at him, his face still set and closed.

'Samuel, my friend,' So-So went on, 'you must not break your son's heart a second time. Trust *me*, trust your *island*, and these black-heart people *will not escape you.*'

Samuel looked at his friend, at Michael, Mr Joseph and Eugenia. His face was set, firm – and then melted. 'OK.' He nodded. 'OK. Let's make a plan!'

Michael thought his father's smile was like the sun coming up over Morne Matin!

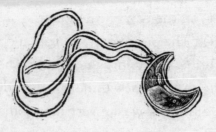

23

Carnival, the very thing that Spargo and JJ
thought would help to cover their tracks so well,
was busy doing just the reverse. That night,
people were up late, making costumes, finishing
floats, talking, drinking, eating, dancing, laughing, sharing, remembering, and just soaking up
the atmosphere. It was as if the entire population
were sharing a dream. And while they did,
the news spread. Not through mobile phones
or computers or faxes, not through orders or
instructions – nothing written or printed. Just
by word of mouth, from one person to the next,
through a touch of the hand, a smile, a frown, a

wink. Almost as fast as thinking, sure and true as a heartbeat.

So that, by morning, everyone understood exactly what the new roads and schools and jobs that Spargo and his shadowy boss and the NME had 'given' them would *cost*. It was a very high price indeed, and they had very nearly been tricked into paying it. Quietly, without any fuss, people decided that being part of a chain of blood, wickedness and misery was *not* what they wanted. Was *not* a price they would pay. Not for *anything*.

And some people looked at the big tank towering over the swanky new quayside and were sorry. And others looked around at the sea and the mountains, at the forest and the streams, and wondered why they'd ever wanted anything more anyway!

All over the island, little things began to happen. First, very early, boats – mostly small, mostly old, mostly with outboards kept going through skill and patience rather than new parts – pulled away from little coves, and headed north on the dream-blue sea. All ready to go as far as they had to.

Then, at telephone exchanges and mobile phone masts, essential wires became mysteriously unplugged, so that soon messages were only travelling in the good old-fashioned way: from mouth to ear. Calling from his whaling ship, the *Ahab*, as he headed north, Spargo couldn't understand why JJ wasn't answering her phone; why even the walkie-talkies crackled and spat but did not speak.

Up at the airport, the shining silver jet, waiting on standby with Spargo's favourite brand of whisky in its drinks cabinet and JJ's favourite perfume in its bathroom, developed an engine fault that meant it was unable to take to the air.

At the breakfast table in the Rathborne Hotel, the coffee that JJ poured was cold, and the toast was burned. When she demanded hot coffee and unburned toast, she was told, very politely, that there was no more. That she had used it all up.

At the fish plant, a hundred women turned up

for work two days early, with a big Carnival float. When the security guards tried to call for help, their phones didn't work, and their guns had mysteriously disappeared, so they were completely helpless when the women loaded the whole safe containing all the new whale-meat packaging onto the float and trundled away down the quayside.

When the Carnival parade finally began its outrageously noisy, joyous progress through the centre of town, JJ took her place on the balcony of the town hall, happy to be known as the head of New Marine Enterprises now that the Fontaines were all safely out of the picture. She smiled charmingly, still believing that everything was going according to plan. But when the NME float, with its free T-shirts and pens showing the NME logo in fluorescent yellow, was replaced by something she had most definitely *not* ordered, she began to realize that something was going horribly, terribly wrong.

A huge sperm whale made of bamboo and paper filled the whole of the New Marine Enterprises float. Mr Joseph, sporting a white beard, stabbed the whale, and it bled red paper blood into buckets with dollar signs on the side; this was collected by friends of Eugenia's dressed up as the fat mayor and the chief of police, with his curly moustache. Eugenia herself played the tall, skinny lady who owned the *Rose Town Gazette* and the radio station.

The people on the balcony with JJ were first dismayed, then angry, then a little frightened, but the crowd below loved it. They cheered and whooped, but when a white sheet unfolded from the balconies of the Happy Flower Hotel and Bar, and a film was projected onto it from the Spice Lounge Café opposite, they fell silent. For the first time in the history of Carnival, the music stopped and everyone was still.

It was a bit wobbly – it had been shot on Samuel's mobile phone – but it showed Michael holding the medallions and the whale-meat packaging. He told the story of the medallions, and of how his own mother, Josephine Jaquard, and Spargo had tied him to a boat and holed her below the waterline.

A microphone appeared in Eugenia's hand.

'Ladies and gentlemen,' she began. Her voice wobbled at first, but only for a minute. She told the crowd all about JJ and Spargo's previous 'businesses', and about their plans for Rose Town as the whaling and smuggling capital of the world. About the whale and the whale boy, and the way he and everyone else on the island had been tricked and lied to.

'We could get rich on this trade of blood,' Eugenia shouted, 'or we could turn away and say to the criminals, the murderers who run it just one word . . .' She turned the microphone to the people, and they shouted that word: 'NO!'

JJ wasn't there to hear it. She was making her way to the airport, not realizing that she would not be leaving on her private jet, but arriving in good time to meet some island police officers who had changed back into their rather unstylish old uniforms to arrest her.

* * *

Michael, Samuel and So-So left Cat's Paw in Mr Dringo's boat before first light. Samuel took the tiller, even though So-So joked that he had forgotten how to steer a boat. They had spare fuel, food and water, and were prepared for a long journey.

None of them had slept, but they were beyond tiredness. They sat looking out on the grey dawn water, the scattered shapes of waking birds, and the line of the horizon materializing out of the dusk, So-So in the prow and Michael with his father in the stern.

Samuel gave a long sigh. 'I hope So-So's right,' he said, 'or I'll be putting you in danger again. We know that Spargo won't think twice about sinking a boat.'

'Will we catch up with them?'

'I don't know, son,' he said. 'If we're on our own, I almost hope not. The *Ahab* is a big ship, and her crew will be armed and used to the worst kind of trouble.'

'Look!' So-So's cry broke into their conversation; he stood in the bow, pointing. 'See, Samuel, my brother, the good word always spreads fast!'

All along the Rose Town waterfront, little boats were heading out towards them, pulling the silky sea behind them in pleats. One, faster than all the rest, scooted across the water and drew alongside them.

'Samuel Fontaine!' exclaimed the old guy at the tiller. 'As I lives and breathes. Where you been, man?'

Michael saw Samuel consider telling the man that he was Daniel Paul, on holiday from South London, but the thought passed, and he smiled his old smile.

'Oh, you know – around!' he said, shrugging. He looked at the young woman in the prow, holding a video camera on her lap. 'I see your girl's grown up!'

'Hi, Mr Fontaine!' said the young woman. 'Remember me? Louise? I live in New York now. Work in TV. So-So promised me a good story!'

Samuel and So-So exchanged a glance.

'You know your course?' So-So asked her father as he pulled away.

'Line up Morne Pierre over Morne Liberty,' the old man called.

'. . . keep going and watch out for rocks!' his daughter added.

Later, as the sun grew hot, the flotilla of little boats rafted up, to share information, food and water. They were almost directly north of the island, and it was clear that their course lay out in the channel. The smallest and frailest craft would have to turn back at that point, but this still left fifty-two boats that would cope with rougher seas as long as the weather held fair.

Louise filmed some of the fishermen talking. They were a little shy, but quite sure that they didn't want a return to killing whales.

'My grandpa told me all 'bout it,' one old chap said. 'Blood and guts and oil. Horrible. The world have moved on since those old days.'

His son added, 'Not many countries have whales. We should be proud that we stopped killing them so the whole world can come to Liberty and see them!'

Louise's dad insisted that she turn the camera on him. 'We may not have skyscrapers and shiny cars,' he said with a smile, 'but we have a green island and a blue sea. What is better than that? We are rich already.'

They set off again, more cautiously now. So-So and the riddle were right: the Lions were tiny islands; a mass of rocks too, hidden just below the surface. Around them the water sucked and eddied with unpredictable currents. The sun was sinking, and they were still navigating their way carefully through the maze, so busy keeping a lookout for obstacles that they nearly missed the big dark shape of Spargo's ship on the horizon.

'There they are!' Michael yelled. 'Quick! We've got to hurry!'

But they weren't yet out of the Lions' mouth, and risked a holing, followed by a rapid sinking.

The flotilla fanned out to find the best route through, but slow and steady was the only way.

By the time they were clear of the rocks and islets and into the Byte itself – the stretch of deep water beyond the Lions – the light was almost gone, and Spargo's monster ship had disappeared. Behind them, Morne Diabolo was obscured by the tall dark shoulders of Morne Pierre, as if this was the only mountain on the whole of Liberty. The flotilla drew together again and kept a straight course over the growing swells and the deep, deep water under their keels. Darkness flushed over the sky from the east, and as it seeped down into the western sky, a row of three stars showed, faint but clear, just a finger's width above the horizon.

They had found the place and the time: Peter hid Diabolo, and the Angels shone on the Lions' Byte – the deep canyon of water that stretched under the stars for five miles in every direction.

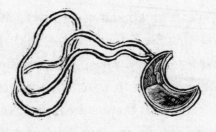

24

The night grew still and calm. The long swells, which had previously rolled them up and down like carts on a fairground ride, died. The bold little boats headed further and further out onto the starlit water, their sleepless, determined crews alert, scouring the darkness for a shape.

Michael stood in the prow listening to the faint fizz of their bow wave as they moved forward. The sea was so calm that it felt as if they were standing still; only the dark mass of the island shrinking behind them gave them any indication of travelling.

There was no sign of the *Ahab*, or of a whale.

Michael began to wonder if they were all – little boats and the *Ahab* too – on a wild, hopeless search. He was almost asleep on his feet, so when the change came to the water around them, he thought at first that he was dreaming.

Clouds of phosphorescent light began to billow and blossom under the surface. Michael knew it was no dream when the other crews began to call out to each other, exclaiming in wonder. One by one they stopped their engines and hove to, somehow knowing that this first gentle flushing of light was only the beginning of what the riddle of the medallion had foretold.

The moving clouds became curtains, shimmering and waving under the water. Then the backdrop of pale light was shot through with intense lines of brightness that glowed for a second or two, then faded. More and more lines, from every angle and direction, shading in the sea with a cross-hatching of green light.

Then, amongst these lines, wide paths appeared, glowed and faded – as if the artist of submarine light had put down the fine pen and taken up a broad, bold brush. The lines, both fine and wide, began to zigzag and bend, so that what had been a cross became a mass of wild, random scribblings.

When the sea around the little boats was covered in gleaming threads and strokes, the whales came up. One after another, and another and another. Their black backs streamed with liquid light, and their spouts exploded into the darkness like fireworks as their breath carried the misted droplets of water and phosphorescence into the air. They rolled and bobbed in the water, showing tails and backs, flippers and flanks. In their jaws were huge squid, bright and glowing so that the whales' eyes caught the light and shone like dots of starlight.

The human watchers were transfixed, as if this was a dream from which they never wanted to wake. The otherworldly beauty and magic of what they were seeing removed all other thoughts and feelings, and they forgot themselves in the joy of this moment.

There's a place where the water runs deep enough to lose the highest mountain. That's where the whales come. So many you can walk on their backs . . .

The shot of the harpoon gun rang out across the water. Michael came back to himself and turned to see the shock and horror on his father's face in the eerie light.

'That's the *Ahab*! Come on!' Michael yelled. 'We've got to stop them!'

Engines fired up all around them, startling the whales and sending them back down; where there had been glowing backs and jaws there were now tails, slicing down into the clouds of brightness.

The *Ahab*'s lights were clear to see now, and the little boats sped across the water towards her. Another shot cut through the night. The approach of the small boats hadn't put Spargo off. Either he thought they were some strange part of Carnival, or he was confident that the islanders still wanted the blood money he was bringing.

Michael stood up in the prow, leaning

forward, trying to urge the boat faster through sheer willpower.

Now the boats drew together, and raced like an arrowhead over the water towards Spargo's ship; and as they approached, Michael could see how huge she was, her sides rising out of the water like some vast building. At the front was the harpoon platform, floodlit, and with huge lights shining down onto the sea below. The unmistakable shape of Spargo himself stood behind the harpoon gun. Lashed to the side of the ship, still streaming with glowing phosphorescent light, were the dark bodies of two sperm whales.

The water in front of the ship was alive with spouts. In the light from the ship the phosphorescence was bleached away, and the backs and heads of the whales appeared extra black, the photographic negative of what they had just seen. Michael counted at least twenty. Further away still were more blows, and tails showing briefly above the surface as the whales went down. At least they would be safe for a while;

perhaps long enough to stop Spargo in his tracks.

The ship showed no sign of slowing down, so the little boats fanned out around her, encircling her as they had arranged. So-So took the tiller of Mr Dringo's boat and pushed the outboard to its limit, bringing the boat close to the *Ahab*, whose crew began to shine spotlights down onto them.

Up ahead, a whale's head broke the surface with an explosive spout, up from a long squid-feasting dive. Even over the sounds of so many engines, Michael heard the flute-like squeak.

Weeepffff!

It was Freedom's mother!

There was a loud bang, and the harpoon, its rope vibrating like a demented snake, shot out over the water, captured in the flat glare of the floodlights. It hit her, and she thrashed her fork-tine tail and arched her body out of the water, spouting blood.

Behind the *Ahab*, one section of the little flotilla had been dropping chains and nets and ropes to catch on the propeller. There was a horrible grating crunch as she was brought to a halt. Everything stopped. The ring of little boats held still, their engines idling. The big ship wallowed helplessly, her engines dead.

Spargo's crew were armed just as Samuel had said they would be. They stood on deck, pointing guns and lights out at the fishermen, but no one flinched, and Spargo knew that shooting more than a hundred and fifty people and sinking fifty-two boats was impossible.

A bright light shone down into Dringo's boat, and Spargo noticed at last who had been leading the pursuit.

'You!' he yelled. 'I should have done for you same as that boy of yours.'

Michael stepped into the floodlight beside his father, and Spargo let out a huge growl of fury, like a chained dog.

'You're finished!' Samuel yelled. 'We know about the whale meat. Interpol are on their way to pick you up.'

'I'll be long gone before they get here!'

'Not with a chain around your propeller, you won't. Bye, Spargo!' Samuel turned the boat and drew away from the *Ahab*.

The whale, Freedom's mother, still thrashed at the end of the rope, though more weakly now. Dying. Michael's heart turned over in pity and sorrow.

'You can't leave!' he yelled. 'He'll just get away!'

'You going to board a ship with an armed crew?' Samuel snapped. Michael hung his head.

'You think I want the man who tried to kill my son to go free?' Samuel continued fiercely. 'He's not going anywhere. With a fouled prop and the current, they'll be on the Lions' Byte by nightfall, holed below the waterline and sinking. He knows it, and his crew know it. What's more, they know the best thing they can do is hand him over the first chance they get. If they take to the lifeboats they'll be picked up the moment they hit land.'

'What about Freedom's mother?' Michael cried.

'There's nothing more we can do for her, son.' Samuel put his arm around Michael's shoulders. 'But let's get back and see what we can do for your friend Freedom.'

They got back to Rose Town at breakfast time, after the quietest Carnival night anyone could remember. Policemen – dressed in their old uniforms – waited on the quay and, after a brief conversation with Samuel, set off in a police launch, with So-So as guide and a boat load of soldiers to arrest Spargo.

Samuel said that as soon as the phones, mobiles and internet worked again, he would be too busy to even think – so, dirty and exhausted as they were, he and Michael went to visit Gran.

She was sitting up in bed in her private room, tiny and fragile as a fairy, but she knew both of them as they walked through the door. She shaped both their names with her lips, although her voice was too weak to speak. They sat on either side of her bed, each holding a hand. She didn't seem to want anything more than that.

Michael thought of the whales lined up and ready to dive, touching flippers. He felt a connection running from the hand he held in his, to the other hand that Gran was holding: a line going through her heart from his to Samuel's. He wanted Samuel not to go away again, but he couldn't ask. But then his father said it for him:

'I won't go back to England, you know.' His voice was flat with tiredness. 'We'll get our boat. Go out on the ocean.'

Michael squeezed Gran's hand, and knew that Samuel would feel it too.

They watched her face. Her smile was so sweet and her forehead smoothed of the worry lines and creases that had crisscrossed it all the time they were both growing up. When her breathing had changed to the familiar purring snore, they left.

'I think she'll be OK,' Michael said happily as they left the hospital.

'Yeah,' Samuel replied. 'Tomorrow, if I can

escape from the paperwork, we'll go up to the house and tidy it, ready for when she comes home.'

But the next day there was no time for anything. The story of the little island and its fight against Big Crime became international news. Louise's video of the crazy harpoon man and the quietly determined fishermen was shown everywhere. The shots of the glowing sea full of whales spread wonder around the world.

Spargo and JJ waited in jail to be flown to London to face trial, and Samuel seemed almost like a prisoner himself, kept working in the island police HQ all day.

Whale experts flew to Rose Town from America, Europe, Canada, India, Australia – everywhere, to try and decide what should be done with the first captive sperm whale on earth. No one wanted to ask the boy who knew the whale best what *he* thought they should do; *he* wasn't an expert, he was just some kid.

Michael tried to get into the MEC to comfort his friend, but they wouldn't let him in. He couldn't understand what they were waiting for – Freedom could have been back in the sea now! He feared that the whale would die of misery before they decided what to do. After anxiously pacing up and down outside the MEC for a few hours, he gave up and decided to go and see Gran. The walk up the hill would help him to think what to do next. He had to get Freedom released; he *would* do it! He just had to work out *how*.

It was lovely afternoon. It had rained in the morning, and everything was fresh and clean. He breathed deep and let the sweetness of the air soothe him.

The lift up to Gran's floor took ages. He stepped out, and knew the moment his feet hit the grey lino: she'd gone. Sister Taylor came up to him, smiling kindly, but he didn't need to hear the words.

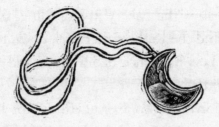

25

She looked younger, more peaceful than he'd ever seen her. He held her hand, but it was cold, like a thing, not a person. Yes, he told the nurses, he would inform her son.

He went down in the lift again. At first he thought the throbbing sensation in the air was just his heart breaking, but it was a helicopter flying so low, the vibration echoed through his whole body. The experts must have decided what to do, and now Freedom would be terrified; it was a helicopter that had begun this long nightmare.

Michael ran all the way past the wooden houses with the sea peeping between, past the public baths, the bakery just opening, the radio station and the Rathborne Hotel, down to where old Mr Levi had once had a shack and a collection of little boats.

He didn't let anyone or anything stop him this time. He simply wriggled out of grabbing hands, slippery as a fish, leaped up stairways too fast for pursuers, and dived head first into Freedom's tank, littered with the remains of fish and squid which the whale had refused to eat.

The water was rank and horrible. Poor Freedom's skin was suffering terribly. He looked frayed. Without even thinking, Michael swam straight towards him, diving down to reach one universe-holding eye. The whale turned at once, that lovely pirouette, so he could look at Michael with both eyes at once, belly up. Then he rose through the water, catching Michael's body on his left side, by the flipper, lifting him as he had once lifted the *Louisa May*, as his mother had once supported the little boat to keep Michael from drowning. Michael rubbed his hand around the whale's eye. He felt the deep trembling as the helicopter hovered overhead, and glanced sideways at the people standing by the tank. He glimpsed their faces for just a fraction of a second, but saw that, at last, they understood and would leave him be. He didn't look at them again, but kept rubbing and stroking, his eyes fixed on Freedom's as the sling was put around them. And together they were carried out of the tank and back to the sea.

The ocean was so sweet after the stagnant water of the horrible tank, its touch as lovely as Gran's smile. Instantly, a shiver of new energy went through the whale. Michael knew that he would be all right. He was weak and afraid, but he was back in his limitless world. Did he know already, just by the sound and feel of the ocean, that his mother was dead? Could he sense the horror still lingering there, even at this distance from the Lions' Byte?

Freedom lay on his side, as he had in the tank, with Michael resting near his left eye, just close enough to the surface to be able to snatch a breath every few seconds. The whale seemed dazed. Then he sank just below the surface. He began to click, as if trying out his voice again, then came back up and breathed: *Pppfffffffffffff* – big and slow, in his own majestic time once more.

Pffffffffffff.

He lifted the curved corner of his snout out of the water, swimming slantwise. Michael remembered that first time, when he thought Freedom was laughing at him. He felt it again now: the whale was telling him, *Weird little land creature, let go of your smallness.* And for a moment Michael did. Freedom pushed his square nose against Michael's body, carrying him around like a limp starfish. And Michael felt the hugeness of the whale, and its oneness with all around it, the same fluid inside and out, up and down and along.

As an adult male sperm whale, Freedom would explore every part of the blue world, every sea and ocean. He would meet humans. Humans like Spargo, like JJ, or just humans too joined to their little land-animal smallness to understand that no one gains anything by harming a whale. To be safe, Freedom must never again be this close to a human being.

Would he feel betrayal? Hatred? It wrenched Michael's heart to think so. And to give up for ever this feeling of connection with so great and gentle and alien a being was a grief almost too great to endure. But love was about doing what was best for the person you loved. So Michael knew that in return for all that Freedom had given him, there was small but invaluable gift he could offer in return.

Mistrust.

He fumbled for the silver half-moon on the string around his neck, pointed and sharp as a tooth. It was too small to do lasting damage to so large a creature, but it would sting, and teach him a lesson: that humans could not be trusted.

It was hard to see with the tears and salt water in his eyes, but Michael drew back his arm and struck out with the silver thorn, as near to

Freedom's sensitive blowhole as his outstretched arm would reach.

A shudder went through the whale. Instantly he tipped the boy off, and turned down towards the safety of the deep, altering his buoyancy with perfect precision. Michael bobbed there on the surface, spluttering, washed in the wake of his tail, as the loveliness of Freedom's strange body receded for ever into the blue.

AFTERWORD

I've been lucky enough to spend time helping with scientific studies of sperm whales in waters off Sri Lanka in the Indian Ocean, off Mexico in the Sea of Cortez and off the Commonwealth of Dominica in the Caribbean, where the idea for *Whale Boy* was born. And every time I see a sperm whale again, their strangeness takes my breath away. They are just so weird! Their huge head always reminds me of the black plastic heating oil, tank that used to sit in my parents' back garden!

But they are also beautiful. Once, a very long time ago, I was – like Michael – in the water with a group of sperm whales. For the first time I saw them as they were in *their* world of water, not just as odd body parts sticking up into *my* world of air. Underwater I could see how their squareness tapered to a tail stock that looked as delicate as the stalk of a leaf. They were *bendy*, like creatures made of rubber, twisting round each other, turning upside down and sideways, moving so gracefully. I was captivated.

Sperm whales not only look remarkable, they *are* remarkable. They are only visitors to the surface of the ocean. Most of their lives are lived one thousand metres down and deeper, a world more alien to us than the moon. To do that, they hold their breath for an hour and more and store oxygen in their blood and muscles. They find their way around in total darkness by echolocation – clicking and listening to the echoes of their clicks. Almost all that huge head is devoted to click-making; it's filled with a kind of oil – spermaceti – that helps them to shape and project their clicks. Clicks are sometimes very loud, louder even than a jet plane taking off, and they can be fast or slow, long or short or come in repeating patterns. Many of them help to give a sound picture of the underwater world and prey. But clicks have another job too: communication. Sperm whales *talk* in clicks. We don't know what they're saying yet – trying to work it out is like trying to break a code – but they might be able to talk about the things that we talk about: emotions, ideas, memories. Certainly they have brains big enough for that kind of conversation – the biggest brains on the planet, in fact.

Sperm whales live in all the world's oceans, wherever the water is deep enough for them. They live in groups of mums and sisters and aunties and their calves, led by old females, and visited every once in a while by big males, who weigh almost twice as much as the females. They form strong relationships and groups stay together for generations. Each group wanders over an area of ocean 1500 kilometres across. Females prefer warmer waters but males travel right up to the edge of the polar ice caps to find food. They travel across oceans, visiting groups of females thousands of kilometres apart.

In the eighteenth and nineteenth centuries, and again in the twentieth, sperm whales were hunted for their oil and flesh. Then, in 1986, the members of the International Whaling Commission, representing countries around the world, banned whaling. But Japan, Norway and Iceland never agreed with the ban and whalers from those countries have killed thirty thousand whales, including sperm whales, since that year. These countries would love to start whaling on a big scale again, but it would take three quarters of the members of the IWC to vote for whaling to overturn the ban. So they try to get small countries in the IWC to vote for whaling by giving them money and help of all kinds. Every year a few more are persuaded. But the tiny island nation of the Commonwealth of Dominica resisted, bravely voting against whaling. Dominicans have never hunted the sperm whales that are regularly found in their waters. They are proud of their whales and now people from all over the world come to see Dominica's sperm whales.

The threat from whaling still hangs over sperm whales and it isn't the only one. Pollution and climate change could reduce their food supply or affect their ability to fight disease. Already they get caught in fishing nets, hit by huge ships, and their hearing gets damaged by the sonar surveying techniques used by the military and oil and gas companies. Sperm whales are highly adaptable and long-lived, but they breed very slowly and depend on their tight social structure for survival. They might be able to withstand one of these threats for a time, but taken together they could mean extinction for sperm whales.

That doesn't *have* to be the ending of this story. We don't *have* to hunt whales or pollute their habitat; we don't *have* to let them drown in our nets or go deaf because of our noise. We can do things differently. We can *change*. We can make sure that sperm whales stay in the oceans for long enough for us to work out what they are talking about.

Just imagine that! It might mean that one day we humans might have someone else to talk to, apart from each other.

If you'd like to help keep whales and dolphins in the ocean, you can join an organisation like the Whale and Dolphin Conservation Society (WDCS). Visit their website for more information: **www.wdcs.org.uk**